INSTRUMENTS OF DARKNESS

INSTRUMENTS OF DARKNESS

T. Ernesto Bethancourt

HOLIDAY HOUSE
New York

Library of Congress Cataloging in Publication Data

Bethancourt, T Ernesto.
  Instruments of darkness.

  SUMMARY: Strange events involving members of
a religious cult headed by a mysterious Rumanian
mystic with incredible powers lead authorities to
suspect a plot to control the world.
  [1. Science fiction] I. Title
PZ7.B46627In   [Fic]   78-11133
ISBN 0-8234-0346-7

To my fellow novelist and friend, Harvey Emerson

And oftentimes, to win us to our harm,
The instruments of darkness tell us truths,
Win us with honest trifles, to betray's
In deepest consequence.

Macbeth
ACT I, SCENE III

Lester Brookman

I want to be sorry. I want to be forgiven. But no one will talk to me. It's as though I didn't exist. I don't know. Maybe I don't. Maybe I died three days ago, and my spirit is still walking the earth. People seem to look right through me. None of the kids in YPI will so much as say a hello. People I know. And people who know me. How can they be so cruel?

Six months ago, during the Love Barrage, I thought I'd found the truth in Brother Ianos. All my life since Mom died, I hadn't been able to get close to Dad. He has the corporation to run. I know he's very busy most of the time. Then I found the YPI. They all loved me! They said so, too. We spent a weekend in the mountains at Brother Ianos' California retreat. It was wonderful. From the moment you wake up in the morning and the last thing at night, you know you are loved. Loved by Jesus, loved by all the YPI's, and especially by Brother Ianos. Then three days ago it ended.

All I said was that I wouldn't ask my dad for anything. I wouldn't sign the letter they wrote. When they told me if I didn't sign, I wouldn't see Brother Ianos again, I thought . . . Well, I don't know what I really thought. Maybe that they'd keep me away from the services.

But not to see Brother Ianos! I can't stand it. I walked right into the services this morning. No one spoke to me. No one acted as though they saw me there. And when he was introduced, I couldn't see him. I sat right down in front and couldn't see him. Everyone around me was saying Amen, as they often do during Brother Ianos' talks. I could hear the amens, but *I could not hear Brother Ianos.* Everyone saw him on the dais. *But I could not see Brother Ianos!* I can't take this. I don't know what I'll do. I keep thinking of what Sister Evelyn said about Judas Iscariot. He hanged himself with a halter . . .

New York Tribune

Another Yippie Suicide

(EDITORIAL, JANUARY 12)

We are the last to discourage any movement that proposes to spread the word of God, as does the so-called Yippie or YPI Church-of-Rumanian holy man, Ianos Iorga. But the reports in the wake of Brother Ianos' Long Walk to New York are not in keeping with the aims of its leader.

In a migration of innocents unparalleled since the Children's Crusade of the Middle Ages, your kids and ours have been joining the swelling ranks of the faithful followers of Iorga on his 3000-mile trek from Southern California to this city. For such a "holy" endeavor, the casualties have been heavy.

The taking of his own young life by Lester Brookman of Los Altos, California, has brought the suicide toll on the Long Walk up to three. Saddest of all is the note young Brookman left: "I could not see Brother Ianos." Six simple words, ending a teen-ager's life.

If this is to be the product of Brother Ianos' Long Walk, neither can this newspaper "see" Ianos Iorga.

Memo

To: Director G.T. Case, Director, I.G.O. HQ, Greenglade, MD.

From: Alvin Gurney, Director, Y Division, FBI, L.A. Branch

Dear George:

Just got a hot communiqué from upstairs about this Ianos Iorga. It seems that Lester Brookman, son of L.B. Brookman, committed suicide while on the Long Walk to New York. This is the third incident of this sort. What distresses us most is that in each case, the kid who killed himself is the child of a man or woman in a position of some sensitivity. Our new director thinks there may be something not quite kosher going on within the YPI movement.

In the new spirit of interdepartmental co-operation in the intelligence community, we'd like to know what you have on Iorga. After all, it was your department that gave him the clean bill of health when he came here from Rumania last year. The President knows of this communication and has requested your co-operation. It would have come directly from our new chief, but the higher-ups feel we can handle this on an informal basis. I await your reply.

Gurney

11

George Case

I'll bet he does. What a riot! Gurney asking favors. When I needed his help five years ago, he told me to whistle. Too bad I can't return his favor and tell him to sit on it. But if the President is requesting co-operation, I guess I have to grit my teeth and open at least part of the files on Iorga. Trouble is, what part? I've met the man myself. And now that I look at my files for last year, I can't believe what everyone said about Iorga, just eighteen months ago . . .

Memo

Via: Diplomatic Pouch

To: G.T. Case, Director, I.G.O. HQ, Greenglade, MD.

From: L.B. Frandsen, Division Supervisor, I.G.O., Bucharest

Re: Ianos Iorga

Dear George:

I'm sure you're aware that this Iorga business is getting out of hand. He's making headlines every week now. Though the current regime here in Bucharest has been tolerant toward the Church of late, it will by no means roll over and play dead if Iorga stays in the headlines.

I think the Party heads underestimated Iorga from the start. You see, there's a long tradition of holy men-come-out-of-the-wilderness here in Rumania. That's all they thought he was. But the man's followers have grown geometrically each week. So have the number of Secret Police assigned to watch him. He may soon become an embarrassment to the Rumanian government. They have their social standing to protect in the Eastern Bloc, you know. And when he does become enough of an embarrassment, that will be the end of Ianos Iorga.

About your question: Can we get Iorga out? My first question is why? Seems to me that Iorga is doing our cause the most good right where he is. That may sound cold from a fellow almost-Jesuit, George, but it's the way I feel. I distrust would-be Messiahs almost as much as I do the Secret Police who always feel they have to do something about them. It seems a shame that only one side of the two can win. And I promise you that it will be the Secret Police.

Anyway, yes. We can get him out. We haven't used the routes and the machinery in years. The political climate has been noticeably warmer in Rumania of late. I suppose I can reactivate the organization in two weeks' time. I'll advise you when all is set. Bear with us. We're out of practice. We haven't played Cowboys and Indians in the Balkans in years.

As to your questions about Iorga, I've never seen the man. I assigned an agent to get me some background on him. He also had an opportunity to hear Iorga speak. I'm enclosing his report. The agent, Nicolae Aricescu,

13

was born in Rumania and came to the States as a child, just before WW II. We put him back in place here shortly after the Cold War began. I don't doubt his loyalty. I doubt his credibility as a witness. I think he was taken in by some very smooth sort of mass hypnosis and communicated hysteria. I have no other explanation for the report you will read. Bear in mind, however, that in the past this agent has been 100 percent reliable. My best to the busy gnomes in the bowels of Greenglade.

Frandsen

Report

To: L.B. Frandsen, Division Supervisor, I.G.O., Bucharest

From: Field Agent Nicolae Aricescu

Re: Ianos Iorga

Sir:

At your request, my report on Ianos Iorga. I presume that this report is for eyes other than your own. It is difficult to believe that anyone living in Rumania would not already know most of the particulars of Ianos Iorga's life.

Ianos Iorga was born about nineteen years ago in the village of Bistrita in Transylvania. Part of the lore about

14

his life is that, prior to the time he was eighteen years old, there was no indication whatever of his divine mission. His father was a farmer; the boy Ianos became a farmer. No strong religious ties. In fact, Iorga's paternal uncle is a Party member and a minor official in Bistrita.

But a few days before young Ianos' eighteenth birthday, he was badly injured. While plowing a field, he fell from the tractor and struck his head on a rock. He lay in a coma for several weeks. Just when his family had given up hope, he began to recover.

When he awoke from the coma, Ianos spoke in tongues. It is said he spoke French, Italian, Spanish. Even English. And Ianos Iorga had never been more than five miles from Bistrita in his life! He had finished elementary school with only the greatest of difficulty. Yet, now Ianos could discourse on philosophy. He could quote entire chapters of Scripture. He knew Orthodox rites. It was a sign of divine visitation.

Once recovered from his injury, Ianos began to walk across the land. Preaching, healing. Within a year, his followers have become legion. I have been privileged to hear Ianos Iorga speak. I fear no ridicule when I say to you that Ianos Iorga is a saint. It is my unspoken belief that he may be even more than that. These are strong statements, but I believe them true.

I saw Iorga in the town of Breaza, which is 103 km. from Bucharest. Though near the Ploesti oil fields, the town is in the mountains and in no way involved with the petroleum industry. Breaza has been a health spa for generations. Its main source of income is tourism. There are many who believe in the curative power of Breaza's waters.

When I arrived, Iorga had already been in Breaza for

two days. Despite the chill of the early April weather, he preferred to live outdoors. He was camped in the foothills outside of town. I reached his camp just in time to hear him speak to the crowds that assembled.

Physically, Iorga is not prepossesing. He is of average height, I would estimate 1.7 m. and weighs about 70 kg. He has dark hair and a full beard; piercing dark eyes. He moves as gracefully as a ballet dancer, but is not effeminate in manner.

He has some trick when speaking to the public that allows him to be heard outdoors in conversational tones. I stood at the rear of the crowd, about 40 m. distant, and heard him as clearly as if he were standing next to me.

When he began to preach, I must confess that I was skeptical. Twenty minutes later, I was among the throng who pressed close, trying to touch his garment. Not that the sermon was inflammatory. Iorga seemed to know even to the tone of voice what would arouse the many Secret Police agents that dotted the crowd like raisins in a pudding.

When questions were asked from the crowd, he took no chances and answered in parables. I believe the men asking the questions were provocateurs. If you wish to know exactly how he handled these men, I can only refer you to the manner in which Christ answered the lawyer of the Pharisees.

Up to this point, I was still somewhat in doubt. But then Iorga did something that can only be described in terms of faith. He healed! He performed a miracle!

At the end of his sermon, a woman brought her young son up to Iorga. She is a resident of Breaza, and I personally checked her history after the Secret Police had done the same. The woman's son had been mute and deaf since birth. Doctors had been of no use. But Iorga put his hands on the boy's head, shut his eyes, and turned his face to the sky. Iorga spoke softly, but I heard him perfectly.

"You will hear my voice," Iorga said.

The child started, as though struck! A bewildered look came over his face. It appeared as though the boy were about to burst into tears. But Iorga soothed him with a touch and said, "You will now speak."

The boy looked at the crowd about him; the faces watching. Slowly, ever so slowly, he opened his mouth. "All praise to God," the child said.

The populace went mad! Anyone with an infirmity, real or imagined, pressed close, crying out to be healed. And as I watched, Iorga cured some twenty people of varying ages. They had illnesses ranging from clubfoot to blindness. He healed them all!

I know that at this point, the Secret Police would have loved to descend on Iorga and take him away. But frankly, it would have taken a company of infantry armed to the teeth. Anyone present would have fought to the death to defend Iorga. Myself included. It is my personal opinion that Iorga is everything his followers make him out to be. Iorga himself denies that he is either prophet or saint. He is firm in his support of the virtues of hard work and obedience. He makes no bones about believing in God. But that's no crime, even in Rumania. I have seen him heal the sick. This man is a saint. May God be my witness!

N. Aricescu

Memo

To: Alvin Gurney, Director, Y Division, F.B.I., L.A. Branch

From: G.T. Case, Director, I.G.O. HQ, Greenglade, MD.

Re: Ianos Iorga

Enclosed is a facsimile of reports by I.G.O. agent N. Aricescu, dated April of last year. This is just about all we have. Please mention the I.G.O.'s co-operative attitude to the higher-ups involved.

Case

George Case

Let Gurney chew on that one for a while. If he thinks he's going to get any more from us without coughing up some data we need, he can forget the whole deal. President or no.

It's the strangest thing. There's something familiar about this file, but I can't say just what. I get a strong *déjà vu* feeling each time I go over it. And then there's the episode of Frandsen's grandson. It sure made a believer out of Frandsen. Let's see, when was that? Yeah, it was about the time we were making plans to get Iorga out. Frandsen met with Iorga at a safe house. Safe for Frandsen that is. Still can't figure out how Iorga shook a squad of Secret Police surveillance experts. In fact, that bothers me. Here he is, an eighteen year old, never out of his home town and he can shake a tail as though it wasn't there. But what is it Frandsen says in his report?

Report

To: G.T. Case, Director, I.G.O. HQ, Greenglade, MD.

From: L.B. Frandsen, Division Supervisor, I.G.O., Bucharest

Re: Ianos Iorga

Dear George,

This man has restored my faith. Aricescu was right, he is a saint. I met with Iorga at Safe House K-3. We spoke only for fifteen minutes. I wanted to make sure that Iorga wanted out of Rumania. I'm aware of the pressure to get him over to our side. It comes from every churchgoer in the States, near as I can tell from the press. I needn't tell you my attitude toward self-styled holy men. But I wasn't prepared for this.

First off, he's hardly more than a boy. He's due to turn nineteen next month. Or we think so. Where he was born, records aren't all that accurately kept. But the aura of confidence and serenity that surrounds him gives him the air of a person many years his senior. I had one of my migraines and almost didn't go. But as it had taken so long to set up the meeting, I decided to fight the pain and went to the rendezvous as scheduled.

Agent Aricescu was present and will bear out what I'm about to set down. Aricescu introduced us. As I took Iorga's hand, I noticed it was hard and calloused; a working man's grip. Firm and dry. I felt a tingling sensation as we touched hands. Then Iorga said to me, "But you are in pain." And George, he said it in English! The reason I had Aricescu along was to act as interpreter on fine points. My Rumanian is all right, but Iorga is from Transylvania, and I know he prefers Magyar. Mine is nonexistent.

I hadn't yet recovered from the shock of Iorga's English, when he sat me down in a chair. He stood behind me, so I can't say how he did it. I felt one of his hands on the top of my head, the other at the base of my neck. It took less than five seconds, and my migraine was gone. I didn't even have the dizziness and letdown I sometimes get after a migraine. I was stunned.

"Better?" asked Iorga.

"Amazing," I replied. "Completely gone. How did you do it?"

Iorga smiled. "I did nothing," he said. "You were healed by God. I am but his instrument—a poor, unworthy vessel."

"Then you do think of yourself as an instrument of God?" I asked.

"Not any more than you are, if you will allow yourself to believe."

"I'm afraid that my faith is a bit rusty," I said. "This is a highly secular work I'm in. Over the years, I suppose my faith has been tempered with cynicism. I rarely see the good in people, and most of my people are . . ."

"They are espionage agents," Iorga put in. "It is a career that by its very nature is based on lies, deceptions and chicanery. But do not feel you cannot return to God. He will accept you as he accepted me, a poor farm boy, raised a good atheist communist."

Iorga got up from his chair and began to walk about the room. He wasn't pacing. Just walking. Then he turned to me and said, "I have decided to leave my homeland. I wish to establish a church in the United States. There is no religious freedom here in Rumania. One day, I shall return to my own country. Then, true faith will rule again."

"And that true faith is what?" I asked.

Iorga smiled at me and said, "I see you have studied your God. From your way of questioning and answering, I should say you were educated by Jesuits. True?"

"True," I said. "University of Loyola in Chicago."

"Then you know the power of faith," said Iorga. "If you will believe, anything is possible. For instance, your grandson. He suffers from epilepsy. He takes daily medication to control seizures. He need take the medicine no longer. He is cured. I will see him as soon as I can after arriving in your country."

The rest of the meeting was taken up with the hows and wherefores of getting Iorga out of Rumania and into Austria. You're well aware of how our network functions; I needn't furnish details. But my point is this: I called my daughter in Georgetown and told her what

21

Iorga had said. She refused to interrupt the medication for my grandson, just on the say-so of Ianos Iorga. When I finally made enough fuss, she had Jimmy re-examined. George, I swear by all that's sacred, the boy's electroencephalograph (E.E.G.) is normal!

In addition, I haven't had another migraine since I met Iorga. As I told you, I think the man is a saint!

Yours in Christ,

Frandsen

George Case

Some turnaround for Frandsen, all right. But I can't blame him. I have to admit that Iorga bowled me over too. Saw him at the White House. No way I could have had him over to Greenglade. The President himself has only been here once. I don't like to think about that time too much. It almost turned out to be the end of the Western World. A Puerto Rican slum kid named Eduardo Rodriguez gained control of our main defense computer, ODIN. But that's past history. Rodriguez is dead. He died when the computer he was controlling by mind power blew up.

But it was scary while it lasted. That Rodriguez kid was a psychic-power adept. He could read minds, control objects, even predict the future. It was only by luck and with help from a civilian psychiatrist named Myra Sokolow that we stopped Rodriguez. By the time we finally brought Rodriguez down, he was already in con-

trol. Even the President was little more than Rodriguez' puppet.

But if the President remembered me, he didn't let
on. He chatted with Ianos Iorga and twice walked by
me without so much as a nod. I guess he'd just as soon
forget about Rodriguez too. Or he was just too involved
with Iorga.

But I won't forget Rodriguez in a hurry. In fact, I still
have one of his boyhood chums watched by my agents.
Not that I'm still worried. I have nothing to fear from
this kid. What's his name? Yeah, Guzman. That was it.

Rafael Guzman

Eddie's alive! I can't believe it. Got his postcard this
morning from California. What's he doing out there?
Does the Man know he's alive? The feds told me that
Eddie was dead. Two years ago. The postmark on the
card says Los Angeles.

Not that anybody but me would know the card came
from Eddie. All it said was ¿*Qué tal*, Rafael? No signa-
ture or nothing. But if I don't know Eddie's handwrit-
ing by now, forget it. I got a bunch of cards from Eddie
a few years back. I saved them; kept them hidden. I put
this new card I just got next to one I've had for years.
No doubt. It's Eddie's writing. I wonder what's happening?

I'll tell you this, though. Whatever Eddie needs or
wants, if I can help, I will. I owe Eddie everything I got.
If it wasn't for Eddie, I'd still be a delivery boy for

Greenberg's market. He got me the bread to buy my store, along with my brother Pablo. Eddie even got me out of the Federal slammer a coupla years ago. But I never got to see him. I was in this joint some place near Washington D.C. for a month. Eddie saw to it I was treated right. He got me a brand-new set of clothes to leave in too. And up until he died a few months back, my dad got a swell government check each month. That was Eddie's doing too. So if he needs anything I got, he can have it. If he needs somebody wasted, he got that too. I'm gonna sit tight and wait to see if he writes to me again.

Memo

Jan. 20

To: G.T. Case, Director, I.G.O. HQ, Greenglade, MD.

From: Secretary of State

Re: Ianos Iorga and YPI Church

It has been brought to the attention of this office that Ianos Iorga's YPI Church has been in some way connected with the recent suicide of L.B. Brookman's son, Lester. If this were an isolated incident, it could be easily ascribed to the actions of a neurotic attracted to still another revivalistic religious cult.

But there have been three suicides in the past two months. In addition to Brookman's son, the daughter of the Dakaman Ambassador to the U.N., Jasmin Bakka, has taken her own life by an overdose of sleeping pills. The son of the King of Iguru, sent here for education at Princeton, took a fall down an empty elevator shaft at YPI's New York headquarters. YPI spokesmen say it was an accident. But to do it, the boy would have had to pry open the shaft door first. At that time, I asked the FBI to look into it, as it does have international ramifications. Next day, I got my only report from the Bureau to date. It disclosed that not a soul in the YPI organization knew a thing about it. All near-witnesses, those who last saw the boy before he fell, tell the identical story. And when I say the identical story, I mean right down to the last punctuation mark and turn of phrase. It's as though they were rehearsed. Something here doesn't sound right. Perhaps the I.G.O. can get some results that the Bureau can't.

As to the legality of your operations within the borders of the U.S. in this matter, the fact that both the countries of Dakama and Iguru are mineral rich, and our allies (at least as of this writing), justifies the I.G.O. stepping in. You will, of course, co-operate with the FBI in this matter. The President has directed their new Chief to permit you full access to their files on the YPI Church and Ianos Iorga. I will expect your preliminary report on this at your earliest.

Memo

Jan. 26

To: Records Division, I.G.O.

From: G.T. Case, Director

Re: YPI Church

Get me complete membership lists on the YPI and all data on background since its inception a year ago. Lists are available from our files. You may get a completer picture from the FBI. This memo will serve as your authorization to requisition copies of the FBI's files. I need this information YESTERDAY.

Case

Memo

Jan. 28

To: G.T. Case, Director, I.G.O. HQ, Greenglade, MD.

From: Records Division

Re: YPI Church and Ianos Iorga

As per your orders, here is the list you asked for. As you can see, the FBI's file was larger than ours. We only have kept records on resident aliens in sensitive areas. The Bureau's list gives us a much different picture. I have underlined certain names on the Bureau's list. You may find them interesting.

George Case

Bet that was Irma Schindler down in Records who wrote that memo. She's got a mastery of understatement. After checking the YPI list, it seems that over 75 percent of the most influential men and women in the Western World have kids in the YPI movement!

Not that it makes them suspect or anything. After all, you can't get upset if your kid wants to join a church and get closer to God. But it also seems to me that a group that controls those kids can bring a whole lot of pressure to bear on the entire Western Bloc, on a U.N. or national level. I think it would help to have the parents of the three suicides interviewed.

Memo

Feb. 1

To: Field Agent J.B. Ortiz, I.G.O., N.Y. Branch

27

From: G.T. Case, Director, I.G.O. HQ, Greenglade, MD.

Re: Jasmin Bakka

You will proceed to the U.N. and interview Selim Bakka, Dakaman Ambassador. Read the enclosed reports carefully. Use standard cover story for your interview. Get a quiet tape, if possible. Report earliest.

Case

Report

Feb. 2

To: G.T. Case, Director, I.G.O. HQ, Greenglade, MD.

From: Field Agent J.B. Ortiz, I.G.O., N.Y. Branch

Re: Ianos Iorga and YPI Church

As per your order, I proceeded to the U.N. to interview Selim Bakka, the Dakaman Ambassador. We met in his office. There was no trouble with my cover as Building Security. But after a few minutes with the man, I realized I was in over my head trying to fool him. He's a career diplomat. I remembered your lecture on initiative in the field, Mr. Case. I took a chance and told him the truth, or as much as was necessary to get what we wanted. I think we got more than we wanted. I ran my briefcase recorder; I don't think he knew. The transcript of that tape accompanies this report.

Selim Bakka is forty-three years of age; about five feet seven inches tall. He is quite thin. He is a very dark-skinned black man. As he was educated at Oxford, he speaks with an accent that is a pleasant combination of Oxonian English and his native Arabic. He is a man of considerable personal charm and was at some pains to put me at my ease. I believe him to be a man of great personal integrity and unquestionable moral fiber. I believe also that all the statements he made in the tape you will read are true, to the best of his knowledge.

Transcript of sub rosa tape # SB 289-410

Subject: S. Bakka

Interviewer: J. B. Ortiz

ORTIZ: Good afternoon, Mr. Ambassador.

BAKKA: Ah, Mr. Ortiz. From . . .

ORTIZ: Building Security, sir.

BAKKA: And what is the latest bit of mischief that brings us together? I assume it must be mischief, actual or potential. In seven years at the U.N., you are the first security person I have met who was not in uniform. My country does not attract the attention of terrorists. Perhaps a sign of our backwardness. Our people are well fed and reasonably happy. But there I go talking, and

29

I'm sure you're a very busy man. Now, how may I help you?

ORTIZ: Actually, Mr. Ambassador, I've come here to try to help you. We have reason to believe that . . . Listen, Mr. Ambassador. I am not really from Building Security. I'm an agent of the International Intelligence Gathering Organization. Here are my credentials.

BAKKA: I see. Then why this security charade? I would have seen you had you identified yourself properly. I don't fear your organization the way some do.

ORTIZ: Well, as you may know, sir, we are not authorized to operate within the continental United States. However, we feel that in a case where international security may be involved, action is justified. There is precedence in the past for this.

BAKKA: Really? What was the situation?

ORTIZ: I'm afraid I'm not free to discuss it, sir.

BAKKA: Then may we discuss what brings you here?

ORTIZ: Of course. We are conducting an investigation into the activities of Ianos Iorga and the YPI Church.

BAKKA: Then this is about Jasmin, my daughter. Forgive me, I don't care to discuss it. Good day, Mr. Ortiz.

ORTIZ: Please, Mr. Ambassador. I took a chance in telling you the truth. I was to have used my cover story as a building security agent. But once we met, I saw that there was no reason to play games. I won't now, either. We believe there may be a connection between the deaths of your daughter, the son of the King of Iguru, and the son of L.B. Brookman, an American industrialist. What that connection is, we don't know. But we're trying to find out. Quietly, before we advise the President to take action.

BAKKA: You may sit down again, Mr. Ortiz. If you will give me a moment to collect my thoughts.

ORTIZ: Of course.

BAKKA: Now, first off, Mr. Ortiz. Do you believe in God?

ORTIZ: Yes I do, sir.

BAKKA: Do you believe in the Devil?

ORTIZ: I suppose I do. I think of God, and I suppose there is an opposite, evil person of some sort. But mostly, I feel it's a . . .

BAKKA: A superstition?

ORTIZ: As good a word as any.

BAKKA: And reincarnation. Do you believe in reincarnation?

ORTIZ: No sir, I do not. I believe there is an afterlife, but not in that fashion; coming back as another person or an animal.

BAKKA: Mr. Ortiz, you consider me a reasonably intelligent and educated man, do you not?

ORTIZ: Indeed I do, sir. You wouldn't hold the government position with your country that you do if you weren't.

BAKKA: Then what I am about to say, you may believe or reject. But do not discount it as the superstition of a man just out of his village, with no experience of the outside world.

ORTIZ: I would never . . .

BAKKA: No assurances, please. Your acceptance of my veracity is enough. Let me tell you about my country so that you may better understand my story. My land has two major populations. Most of the people in the cities are followers of Islam. In fact, almost all the people in government are Islamic. But the

31

people of the back country have a different religion. In the name of ambition and a certain amount of belief, I embraced Islam some twenty-four years ago. I am from the back country. I have not forgotten the way I was raised. Enough to say that I do believe in a Devil, reincarnation, and possession of humans by demons. It is not a superstition. It is my religion, or was.

ORTIZ: I think I understand.

BAKKA: It's enough to keep an open mind. Now as to my daughter. I last saw her three weeks before she . . . died. She was completely wrapped up in Christianity. Or at least Brother Ianos Iorga's variety of it. I was unhappy about it but blamed myself. After all, had I not turned my back on my own childhood religion? Was this a proper example for my only child?

ORTIZ: Did she seem unhappy or distressed? Or was there a quarrel between you about it?

BAKKA: Forgive me if I anticipate you. No, there was nothing between us that would have prompted her to take her life. She was ecstatic about her newly found faith. She was euphoric.

ORTIZ: Euphoric in the sense of drugs, sir? Excuse me for asking.

BAKKA: It is not necessary to apologize. I answered the same questions from the California police when she died. It's a good question, considering the drug culture among young people in your country. No. She did not appear to be drugged. Jasmin never took medications except for antibiotics prescribed when she was ill. That was not the nature of her euphoria. It was a religious ecstasy, as may be seen among dervishes in Africa. I knew it for what it was.

ORTIZ: Then, what would you say her mental state was?

BAKKA: She was possessed by a demon.

ORTIZ: I beg your pardon?

BAKKA: As I said. She was possessed by a devil. I believe that that devil reincarnated is Brother Ianos Iorga. He had claimed her soul.

ORTIZ: But you said she was happy. Even ecstatic. Hardly a sign of possession.

BAKKA: Do you know the signs so well?

ORTIZ: No, sir. I mean that from all I've read, films I've seen . . .

BAKKA: You mean the claptrap in sensational films? Nonsense! If possession were so terrible a thing to the possessed, it wouldn't happen as often as it does. And I believe that possession is much more common than you think, Mr. Ortiz.

ORTIZ: But outward signs of distress. Surely there would have been such signs.

BAKKA: Why should there? When a demon or devil takes residence in a human, it offers the human something in exchange. Favors, riches, power. This devil that possessed my Jasmin is a modern devil. He offered her what your entire nation pursues with such joyless vigor. He offered her happiness and joy in *this* world, not the next. Think, Mr. Ortiz. If someone or *thing* offered you ecstatic happiness for the rest of your life, would you consider it?

ORTIZ: I don't think so, sir. My training, my religion would keep me from being sucked in.

BAKKA: And if this devil came to you in the guise of a holy man, a Christian, like yourself?

ORTIZ: That's different. I think I'm beginning to see

33

what you mean. But in that case, sir, how could you tell the difference between demonic possession and true religious fervor?

BAKKA: You can't. And for good reason. Possession and righteous fervor are both forms of religious conviction. The possessed are worshiping a different deity. The outward signs are the same: utter and unshakable belief.

ORTIZ: Then how did you spot it in your daughter, sir?

BAKKA: May the heavens help me, I didn't recognize it. I saw that Jasmin was confirmed in her new Christianity and appeared so happy, I did not intervene. It was not until after her death that I found out. I thought her fervor would pass after a time, and that she would return to me. I did not want to drive my daughter from me by taking a stand against Ianos Iorga.

ORTIZ: You say after her death you found out. How?

BAKKA: She left a suicide note for me. It was brought to me when the police were done examining it.

ORTIZ: I've seen a copy. It's almost identical to the one young Lester Brookman left. The key phrase appears to be *I could not see Brother Ianos.*

BAKKA: That I would not know. But at the bottom of the page, in a corner, there was one word written in Arabic, though the note was in English. I think it was missed because Jasmin's Arabic is poor. She has grown up speaking English for the most part. The word was probably taken for a scribble on the page. But I did not miss it.

ORTIZ: What was the word, sir?

BAKKA: The word was *Shaitan,* Mr. Ortiz.

ORTIZ: Which means?

BAKKA: It means Satan, Mr. Ortiz. The Devil himself!

George Case

Swell can of worms. One of my top men turns into a New Christian and calls Iorga a saint. Maybe even a Messiah. The U.N. ambassador from Dakama thinks Iorga is the Devil himself! This file gets screwier each day. Frandsen is usually reliable! He's been with the Organization for twenty years. He was graduated from training while I was still giving courses at Greenglade. But Selim Bakka is no savage out of the bush. He's a responsible, intelligent, educated man in a heavy-weight position. Both in his own government and on committees at the U.N.

When I saw Iorga at the White House reception, I wasn't impressed one way or another. But then again, I was paying more attention to the President than to Iorga. But I did file a memo on the reception. Maybe I ought to see exactly what I said in it. It was almost eighteen months ago that I filed my memo. Let's see what it says.

Memo

To: Secretary of State

From: G.T. Case, Director, I.G.O. HQ, Greenglade, MD.

Re: Ianos Iorga

Dear Mr. Secretary:

As you were occupied in the Middle East at the time, I attended the informal reception for Ianos Iorga at the White House. I was greatly impressed. He has an air, an aura of inner peace that he communicates to all around him. I have seen documentation of his healing by faith. The evidence is indisputable. I was prepared to be skeptical, but a few minutes in the presence of this truly *good* man convinced me. If there is a subterfuge in progress, I can't spot it. It just may be that what Iorga's followers say is true: He may well be a saint!

Respectfully,

Case

George Case

I said *that?* I can't believe it! But there it is on the paper, looking right back at me. A saint? Wait a minute. Isn't that what Frandsen said? I just looked at the file again. Cover to cover. This saint or Messiah business keeps cropping up. It's in every eyewitness account and every interview with Iorga. Now I know very well that I don't think Iorga is a saint. In fact, I'm beginning to smell a large, large rat . . .

Anda, Crown Prince of Iguru

I cannot do what Brother Ianos asks. I will not impose upon my father, the King, nor my people. The wealth of my land is still in the discovery stages. I do not know this man, Saunders. I do not know what connection he has with Brother Ianos, save that he too believes. I am torn. I can resist but feebly. My father, the King, could advise me. But I cannot reach him. I have tried. Each time I try the telephone, all I can hear is Brother Ianos' voice. It tells me to write the letter. I cannot do this. But may Jesus help me, what will happen when I am king? My father is an old man. Then Brother Ianos and this man Saunders will control my country's wealth. Yet, I believe in Brother Ianos. I can't stand this pressure. If I cannot live as a true ruler of my people, I can at least die as one.

Los Angeles Chronicle

Brother Ianos Will Accept Orange Co. Land and Building

ANAHEIM, February 12—Speaking to an overflow crowd at the Convention Center, the internationally renowned holy man of Rumania, Ianos Iorga, formally accepted a gift from oil millionaire Edward Saunders, which he had declined earlier.

Saunders has donated a forty-room mansion on a fifty-acre plot of land in the heart of the Southland, close to the town of Santa Amelia. The house will be used as a shelter for the tens of thousands of believers who have journeyed far to see Mr. Iorga and lack funds for public lodging.

This is the second major gift of real estate donated to the YPI Church. The other is the former Viking Hotel on Manhattan's West Side in New York.

The gift of the Santa Amelia house and land merely formalize a *de facto* relationship. Iorga and his followers have been using the premises on a temporary basis since last spring when Iorga arrived in California from Rumania.

The donor, Edward Saunders, noted in the past for his reticence with the Press, made a simple statement of explanation to this reporter. "The man is a saint," he said.

Juan Bernardo Ortiz

Maybe I should have put it into my report. I wonder. I don't want to jeopardize my standing with the Organization. I've only been back on full duty for a little over a year now. And if Case thinks I'm turning flaky, that'll be the end of Johnny Ortiz' career with the IGO. They'll ship me to the Organization's sanitarium in New Mexico again. Oh, I'll be well cared for and fed. They just won't trust me to write with anything sharper than crayons. And my father will get my pension. Not that he needs it. It wouldn't pay the water bill on his place in East Hampton.

I have to face it. I know too much to crack up. I know that the ODIN computer is now a pile of junk in Greenglade's basement. I know how Eddie Rodriguez almost ruled the world by taking over ODIN. And taking over *me* to do it!

I still have nightmares about that. Dr. Elbert in New Mexico said that they'll pass in time. But I can't shake this creepy feeling. There's a sameness to this case that brings back the entire affair with Rodriguez. It was what Bakka said about possession. He had no way of knowing he was talking to someone with firsthand experience. I still feel dirty inside from it! What was it Bakka said about the way all the YPI kids refer to Iorga? They all recite it like parrots: *Brother Ianos is a saint.* And with a blank look and flat tone that makes them sound like tape playbacks.

But who can I tell? I wish I could reach my kid brother, Luis. Seems funny that any time I'm in deep water, I call out for my baby brother. Lou is not what you'd call an average kid. He's only sixteen and doing graduate work at M.I.T. I remember when he was in diapers! Any time Lou has had a hunch, he's been right. I've been calling his number all evening. I don't think the kid ever sleeps. Not that I worry about where he is. Lou can take care of anything that comes his way.

If I breathe a word to Case, I'm off to New Mexico. Wait! Maybe I can reach Dr. Sokolow and Dr. Grossman. They were there when it happened. I know her phone is clean. No one's been tapping that line for over a year.

Martin Grossman

Johnny Ortiz, of all people! Myra and I haven't seen him since the I.G.O. sent him off to their place out West for extended therapy. He was lucky to have recovered as well as he did. The Russian foreign minister, Dimitri Gangov, whose mind Rodriguez controlled for a few seconds, is still being fed by spoon. The profound shock of being controlled by an outside mentality completely unbalanced him.

I wonder what Ortiz wants? I don't think it's I.G.O. business. He wouldn't have made an appointment for such a strange hour, 5:00 A.M. It's about the only time in New York when there's hardly anyone around. He wants to keep his visit quiet for some reason. Myra said Ortiz wants to see us both. That must mean it pertains to the Rodriguez affair. It's the only experience we have in common.

George Case

I know this is going to seem strange to him after all these years, but I'm going to write to Brother Paul. Last I heard, he was teaching at Fordham. Maybe I'm too impressed with all this recent interest in possession—the books and films. But I do know that possession is one of the explanations possible for the actions of these kids that killed themselves. If you accept the idea that possession does exist. The Church recognizes it. But if I take an unformed hunch like this and run it past the Big Boys, I'll be collecting my pension by next Wednesday. I know. I'll keep it on a personal basis. Write him a letter and arrange for an eyeball on neutral ground in D.C. some place.

Paul Sullivan

Dear George,

How many years has it been? I think we both were kids. Delighted to hear that your career with the government has turned out so well. I can't believe that one of my students is now head of the entire Securities Information Bureau in Washington.

I'd love to meet with you. My teaching duties here at Fordham are such that I can get away over the weekend of the 6th. I'll arrive at Dulles on South Coast Airlines, flight 321-A, at 8:30 P.M. the night of the 5th.

Of course I can bring the library texts on exorcism. Why? Are you interested because of intellectual curiosity? Or do you merely have some international stock issue that can't be explained? Forgive me, George. Lately, it seems that people have been spotting Our Enemy under the bed and in closets everywhere. It distresses me greatly. Men seem reluctant to accept the consequences of actions taken while exercising their own God-given free will. It becomes easier to blame

The Enemy. What is it that the T.V. comedian used to say? *The Devil made me do it.*

Anyway, I will take you up on that steak dinner at the restaurant off Capitol Hill that you mentioned. You say they serve a real yellow *Sauce Béarnaise* with the *entrecôte?* Worth a flight to our nation's capitol, anytime. I look forward to seeing you.

Yours in Christ,

Paul

Martin Grossman

I pray that Myra is wrong. But she so seldom is. I've given up resisting when she gets an idea of this scope. Ortiz came to the appointment on time. Myra and I were having coffee when he rapped at the door. Which is a spooky feeling if you're a New York apartment dweller. I.G.O. agents, like lovers, laugh at locksmiths. He probably let himself into the lobby entrance and came directly up the stairs. Didn't use the elevator; we'd have heard it. I wondered initially what all the secrecy was about. Now, I wish I didn't know.

He was quite agitated. Not that a casual observer would have known. I.G.O. trains their people well. And Johnny Ortiz is one of their brightest young men. He looked every inch the young executive. European-cut suit, Cardin raincoat, Gucci shoes. He also was carrying the same air of anxiety so many of our young execs do.

Each time I see Myra at work, I marvel at her abilities. She always was a brilliant doctor. But a few years back, during the Eddie Rodriguez crisis, Rodriguez somehow turned her into a telepath. He had ideas of making her his consort when he ruled the world. So, for his personal convenience, he bestowed this gift upon Myra.

Back then, Myra told me it felt as though Rodriguez had "thrown a switch" inside her head. From then on, she could read the thoughts of others. We've kept it our secret. Well, actually, the retired head of the I.G.O., Darryl Henskey, knows about it. But his successor, George Case, hasn't an inkling of Myra's true powers.

Myra and I have had remarkable success treating executives under heavy stress. The fact that Myra already knows what's troubling a client doesn't make treatment a formality. That is only half the fight. The patient must realize it too. But I'd estimate that the time saved in establishing rapport and being able to spot evasions instantly represents a saving in couch time of easily 50 to 65 percent.

We work as a team. I'm sure that many of the clients think I'm some sort of inarticulate, or Myra's recording secretary. To them, Myra does all the talking. I only speak when she addresses a question or remark directly to me. And my speaking is simply a device at sessions. Myra and I communicate and confer telepathically during the session, unknown to the client. We also tape the sessions and confer more fully afterwards.

I still haven't worked out a form for transcribing these tapes. The sessions are on two levels: vocalized and telepathic. I've been breaking the transcripts down into two-column pages. As when Ortiz arrived:

Vocal	Telepathic
MYRA: Johnny. So good to see you again. How have you been?	(Martin, he's terribly upset.)
ORTIZ: Not too good, Dr. Sokolow. Those dreams have been coming back. How are you, Dr. Grossman?	(True. But that's not why he's come here.)
ME: Fine, Johnny. You say the dreams are recurring? What are they like?	(He's terrified. This boy is on the verge of a breakdown!)
MYRA: Before you speak, Johnny, have you spoken with your doctor in New Mexico?	
ORTIZ: No, I haven't. The time difference. I had to speak to someone right away. Someone who knows . . . what happened to me two years ago.	(He's afraid they'll think he's relapsed and will institutionalize him again, Martin.)

MYRA: Very well, Johnny. But remember, I am not your doctor. I gave you some emergency treatment back then, but I may not interfere with the course of your doctor's treatment. Understood?

ORTIZ: I understand.

(He wants to ask us to keep this meeting confidential. Let's hear what this is all about.)

MYRA: I will mention nothing of this to anyone if you prefer.

ORTIZ: I'd appreciate that, Dr. Sokolow.

(He's loosening up a bit now.)

I sat in horror as the story unfolded. Myra listened carefully, only asking questions to ease Ortiz' tensions. After all, she already knew the answers. It may be that Ortiz' suspicions are unfounded. But Myra thinks he's right. The question is, what do we do about it?

There is no doubt that Ianos Iorga's YPI recruiting methods are textbook examples of mind control. They take any alienated young person, offer him complete loving acceptance, and give him a taste of religious/suppressed sexual ecstasy. They impress on the young person that this feeling can only be attained in conjunction with the YPI Church and Ianos Iorga. Once they're imprinted this way, you can turn them loose. No chains, no threats. You own them.

I especially noted the practice of what the YPI calls the Love Barrage. A kid is taken to one of the YPI retreats. These are always far removed from any of the kid's emotional and cultural roots. If the subject is from the east, they ship him off to the retreat in California. If the subject for control is from the west, they send him to the center in New York.

But the key is isolation and supplanting of the subjects' values in an atmosphere of complete acceptance and love. With so many alienated young people today, there's an unlimited supply of potential zealots. Take the three young people whose deaths Ortiz has been investigating.

Lester Brookman: Seventeen years of age. Father a major industrialist. Mother deceased. Boarding schools. All the material advantages. No parental love or acceptance. Isolation from his father because of the father's business. The poor kid was a sitting duck for Iorga's people.

Anda, the Crown Prince of Iguru: Nineteen years old. Raised completely apart from parents. Royal tutors. The King with many wives. No contact with mother after age six. Feelings of rejection/competition toward the King. He would have succeeded to the throne. Being educated at Princeton, he was already under pressure to adopt values different from those of his upbringing in East Africa. Again, fertile ground for the YPI.

Jasmin Bakka: Seventeen years of age. Father a career diplomat. Mother deceased. No firm religious convictions. Her father a convert to Islam, which he adopted for reasons of ambition. Raised in boarding schools internationally. Poor kid. She didn't have a chance.

The most frightening part of all this is the secular aspect. There are other evangelical religions out recruiting in this fashion. True, they milk the kids of their parents' money. But the bite is rarely grievous enough to cause waves with something like the I.G.O.

For the most part, the other groups do preach love, obedience, respect, and adherence to a Christian or non-violent ethic. But these YPI's are different. When Ortiz told me the figures on how many VIP's children are involved with Iorga, I saw the pattern too. It appears to be an attempt to control the entire Western world through our children!

Washington Dispatch

South Coast Jetliner Falls

DULLES INTERNATIONAL, February 5—A South Coast Airlines jet-liner, carrying one hundred fifteen passengers, crashed and exploded while landing at 8:30 P.M., Friday.

Miraculously, there were some eighty-seven survivors. Flight 321-A from New York had been making a routine approach to land, when inexplicably the huge jet nosed down and crashed on the landing strip. Prompt action by airport fire crews reduced the death toll greatly.

A list of survivors has been withheld as well as names of the dead, pending notification of their families.

Company officials declined to speculate on the cause of the tragedy, until the Federal Aeronautics Administration completes an investigation.

George Case

Two on the same plane! Brother Paul and Johnny Ortiz. And my fault that Brother Paul was on the plane to begin with. On my lousy hunch, a man like that is dead. What's worse, I lied to him about who I am and what I do nowadays. It's a small consolation to me that if there was ever a man in good standing with his God when he died, it was Paul Sullivan.

It's going to be tough explaining this one to the Ortiz family. That kid had nothing but bad breaks all the time he was with the Organization. First a year at the sanitarium in New Mexico; now this. He said he was on to something concerning the Iorga case too. Didn't want to discuss it on the scrambler phone. Only an eyeball would do. If he put any of it in writing, it'll still be in his briefcase. The Organization did a good job on making those things fireproof. I'd better pull Ortiz' persfile and get the family on the phone.

Memo

Feb. 7

To: G.T. Case, Director, I.G.O. HQ, Greenglade, MD.

From: Field Agent Linda Maxwell, Section T, HQ, Greenglade

Re: Field Agent J.B. Ortiz

Using cover of F.A.A. investigation, I sorted through the collected wreckage of South Coast Airlines flight 321-A. Object was to locate the briefcase carried by Field Agent Ortiz. F.A.A. is also interested in the same piece of Organization equipment. From the black box, they're pretty sure that the pilot on the flight had a seizure of some sort during landing. Possibly a coronary. But the cause of the fire and subsequent explosion was not fuel leaking from ruptured tanks. They're what exploded, but the fire began first. F.A.A. sleuths say that the very source of the blaze was Ortiz' briefcase! They feel it was an incendiary device. I stayed mum. I have no way of knowing whether Ortiz was carrying such a device on Organization business. Both the briefcase and Ortiz were charred beyond recognition. A puzzling bit. Aren't all those cases fireproof?

Maxwell

Western Union Telegram

FEB. 5
RENALDO ORTIZ 14 MOCKINGBIRD LA. EAST HAMPTON
NEW YORK

WE REGRET TO INFORM YOU THAT WHILE IN PURSUIT OF HIS DUTIES WITH THE INTERNATIONAL SECURITIES INFORMATION BUREAU YOUR SON JUAN BERNARDO

WAS INVOLVED IN A FATAL AIR CRASH AT DULLES IN-
TERNATIONAL AIRPORT THIS DATE. BUREAU REGULA-
TIONS ALLOW FOR OFFICIAL FUNERAL SERVICES AND
BURIAL AT ARLINGTON. PLEASE ADVISE THIS OFFICE OF
ARRANGEMENTS.

G.T. CASE, DIRECTOR

Renaldo Ortiz

Now this. My poor son! So dedicated to his job. First it
drove him to a breakdown, then it killed him. If only he
could have joined me in the business. But that wasn't
Juanillo's way. A civil servant. Oh, I was proud. I
thought perhaps the federal job would one day lead to
a career in politics. But dead at twenty-three. Dear
God, is there no way I can make my children's lives
safer and better? What good is all the money I've made
if I lose my true wealth, my children?

This man, Case. He said on the telephone Juanillo
was killed in the line of duty. Friday night at 8:30? What
kind of duties were these? To keep a young man at
work when he should have been out enjoying his life—
his youth? It is too late for Juanillo. But by all that's
sacred, I shall see that they will have no more of my
sons, this government.

If Luis expresses a casual interest in anything to do
with the government, this time I will interfere. Not that
anything I say makes a difference to Luis. I don't understand the things he studies up there in Boston. I don't

like the idea of him attending a college when he's only sixteen. Is it part of *gringo* life to rob children of their childhood?

I am tempted to take that offer I got for the business last year. I would move Luis and Angelita to Puerto Rico with me. What do I need the firm for now? Juanillo wasn't interested in wholesale groceries; Luis wants to be some kind of scientist. And all Angelita can think about is that Mercedes she wants so much.

Each day when I drive into the city, I see my sign. It mocks me: EL GRECO FOODS, WHEN ONLY THE BEST WILL DO. Well, I have built the firm. And the best I can do is go to Washington and bury my son.

George Case

What a monstrous inconvenience. Ortiz' father wants to meet me. Now I have to go over to the dummy office in the district. It's really a farce. Anyone in the intelligence community, on either side, knows who I am and what I do. So I must go through this game playing and pretend to his father that Ortiz worked as a securities investigator.

It's doubly a shame because Ortiz already had one decoration for his bravery in the Rodriguez affair. The only people who ever see our departmental decorations are those in the Organization. And this Renaldo Ortiz won't be easy to fool, either.

He's a tough cookie. Self-made millionaire. He started out thirty years ago with a broken-down truck, selling produce on the street. Today, he owns El Greco Foods, the biggest Spanish grocery firm in the country. All on a less than high school education.

He evidently also has raised his three . . . no, it's two now, children by himself for the past sixteen years. His wife died giving birth to the younger son, Luis. Put Juan through Columbia. The daughter, Angela, got bounced out of Sarah Lawrence last semester. Not paying attention to her studies.

This younger son is something else, though. Graduated high school when he was twelve; he's doing some kind of advanced study now at M.I.T. Brilliant kid, evidently. In fact, a pretty good score for the whole family, except for the girl. But two out of three kids turning out that way? I know if I was Renaldo Ortiz, I'd be very proud of my kids.

Transcript of Interview at D.C. Decoy Office

Feb. 10

Subject: Termination of Field Agent Ortiz (719-47-62) in action. (Standard family interview).

Organization Representative: G.T. Case, Director, I.G.O.

In standard procedure for terminated agents whose families are ignorant of agent's true occupation, I met with Renaldo Ortiz, father of terminated Field Agent

J.B. Ortiz. The senior Ortiz was accompanied by his younger son, Luis Jesús Ortiz, aged sixteen years, student at M.I.T.

I gave the usual lecture on how tragic accidents occur in the most innocent lines of work. Had a few dicey moments explaining Agent Ortiz' breakdown two years back. But smoothed it over well. Ortiz' father declined to accept the death benefits and pension due to all survivor's families. Arrangements were made for burial of Agent Ortiz at Arlington National Cemetery, four days from this date.

I had presumed the interview over. The Ortizes had left. I was preparing to leave for my real office at Greenglade when the younger Ortiz returned to my office. After a few seconds, I realized it might be necessary to tape the proceedings. I cut on the recorder with my foot switch, which is why the transcript begins in mid-sentence.

CASE: I don't understand what you're getting at, Mr. Ortiz.

ORTIZ: Oh, I think you do, Mr. Case. All too well. I said that this isn't really your office. It's a dummy setup.

CASE: A dummy office? Really, Mr. Ortiz.

ORTIZ: Yes, really. Look at your desk. There's dust on the keys of the intercom. Look at the panels around the light switches. No finger marks, scratches, or any sign of use. When you used the pen from the desk set before, it was out of ink. You had to use a pen from your pocket . . .

CASE: Have you ever seen a desk set pen that had ink in it?

ORTIZ: Rarely, I admit it. But usually, someone who

53

really uses the desk doesn't have to use a pen from his pocket. He has one in the desk. I also notice that on a Friday, you don't have an item in your in-tray dated before today. You're quite a worker, Mr. Case.

CASE: I like to keep abreast of my work.

ORTIZ: Then there's the fact that the carpet on your floor has no tracks.

CASE: No what?

ORTIZ: Tracks, worn down areas in the carpet nap where there's heavy traffic. Like from the door to your desk. No, you can't bull me, mister. This office isn't in regular use.

CASE: As a matter of fact, I haven't been here too much lately. I . . .

ORTIZ: Do me a favor, Mr. Case. Don't insult my intelligence, and I won't insult yours.

CASE: Just a minute here. I don't have to take this from a kid.

ORTIZ: You took away my brother from me and my family. Then you give us some cock-and-bull story about stocks and bonds. A poor trade for a life. Then, we're supposed to go away like good, law-abiding citizens and say, "Oh, isn't it too bad about Johnny." Well, I happen to know that Johnny was some kind of a spook. And I'm pretty sure that you were really his boss too. I think you're the head spook around here. And your real office is in Maryland, across the river somewhere.

CASE: Oh, really, Mr. Ortiz. This is all so farfetched. Have you been reading too many comic books?

ORTIZ: I last read a comic book when I was four years old, Mr. Case. The most recent book I've read is on quantum mechanics. And that, just to check out some mistakes the author made. I'm writing my own book.

Listen. You are not going to put me off with the age thing. Yes, I am only sixteen years old, but I already have my degree in physics and am working on my doctorate at M.I.T. In all aspects, I am an educated, functioning adult. I'm saying don't try to snow me. I'm on to you and your spy setup.

CASE: I take it that you and your brother spoke of his work, then.

ORTIZ: You take nothing of the sort. Johnny wouldn't have breathed a word. I don't think you could have got it out of him with hot irons.

CASE: Then this is all conjecture on your part.

ORTIZ: Almost all. But a couple of years ago, when Johnny had that breakdown, his briefcase was still at our house on Long Island. Locked, of course. So, I opened it.

CASE: You what?

ORTIZ: I opened it. Don't look so shocked. It wasn't hard. Oh, you must be wondering about the destruct mechanism. Why didn't the case go up in smoke when I opened it? I knew the device was there when I put it under my fluoroscope. Down in my basement workshop. Once I saw the lead lining and the double mechanism on the lock, I put two and two together.

CASE: There's a double combination on those briefcases.

ORTIZ: Child's play. It's a simple three-digit lock with a code reversal. I listened to the tumblers on a contact microphone. Then I ran the whole problem through my calculator/computer and came up with the combination. I must admit though, the code reversal was tricky. I just guessed at that.

CASE: You could have been injured. Even killed!

55

ORTIZ: Then we *are* admitting the briefcase was booby-trapped. Does a securities agency need that kind of stuff?

CASE: I admit nothing, Mr. Ortiz. Do all these questions have a point? Just what is it you want of me, Mr. Ortiz?

ORTIZ: I want to know who killed Johnny.

CASE: South Coast Airlines killed your brother, Mr. Ortiz. Along with a number of other innocent people. There was a Jesuit priest on the flight too. Maybe someone was after him. This is getting foolish, Mr. Ortiz. And I have work to do. If you'll excuse me.

ORTIZ: If you have work to do, it's not at this office. Besides, I have a message for you from Johnny.

CASE: You what?

ORTIZ: A message. Johnny phoned me two days ago. He said that if anything happened to him, I was to go to Washington D.C. and see a man named George Case. I was to give him this message: NIETZSCHE.

CASE: What?

ORTIZ: That's the message. One word: NIETZSCHE. You know, as in the nutty German philosopher.

CASE: I know, I know.

ORTIZ: I've delivered the message, Mr. Case. But I still want to know who killed Johnny? Who or what is NIETZSCHE?

CASE: You have this fixation that your brother was killed. It was an airplane accident. That's all.

ORTIZ: In that event, I guess I'll just go to the *Washington Post*. They might be able to get somewhere.

CASE: Come back and sit down, Mr. Ortiz.

ORTIZ: You'll talk?

CASE: I'll talk enough for you to understand why you

shouldn't go to the *Washington Post.* If my explanation isn't enough, I'll have you jailed on some charge or another until the matter is settled.

ORTIZ: Ah, the land of the free. You could have me jailed?

CASE: You'd better believe it.

ORTIZ: I'm afraid I do. That's the scary part.

CASE: All right, Mr. Ortiz. Your brother worked for an intelligence agency, of which I am an officer.

ORTIZ: That agency being nameless, of course.

CASE: Correct. John Ortiz was en route to Washington to bring me some information on an investigation he was conducting at my order. The plane he took crashed. He was killed. His report was destroyed.

ORTIZ: What caused the crash?

CASE: I'm not the F.A.A. How should I know? I'm waiting for the report now. The prelims indicate that the pilot had some sort of seizure. Possibly a heart attack. It happened at a point in landing where it was too late for the co-pilot to take over, evidently.

ORTIZ: I thought that pilots were all in top shape. They have regular exams, don't they?

CASE: Yes, that's the law. But many a man gets a clean bill of health from his doctor, then has his first and fatal coronary. It happens. Are you satisfied now, Mr. Ortiz?

ORTIZ: If what you say is so, yeah.

CASE: I swear to you it's so.

ORTIZ: If you were covering up state secrets, you'd swear to a lie, wouldn't you, Mr. Case?

CASE: I might.

ORTIZ: Then you might be lying now.

CASE: I might. But I'm not.

ORTIZ: Okay, Mr. Case. I think you've been as straight with me as you had to be, under the circumstances. You're obviously telling me only what I need to know. And I appreciate the fact. Face it, if what Johnny knew got him killed . . .

CASE: Hold on, now . . .

ORTIZ: I'm not saying it did. I'm saying *if. If* what Johnny knew got him killed, I'd be in danger, knowing the same thing. I think you should know this: It doesn't frighten me. If someone did in my brother, he's going to pay for it. Heavy. And if I don't hear from you that whoever's responsible has paid for it, I'm going to start my own investigation. I'll wait for your first report to me.

CASE: I don't report to any snotty kid! I report to . . . my superiors.

ORTIZ: Close. You almost said something. You ought to watch your temper. You could have one of those first and last heart attacks you tell me about.

CASE: You'll hear from me.

ORTIZ: Good. By the way, who's NIETZSCHE?

CASE: None of your business, Mr. Ortiz.

ORTIZ: Okay, okay. Good afternoon, Mr. Case.

CASE: *Goodbye,* Mr. Ortiz.

(END TRANSCRIPT)

Memo

Feb. 10

To: A.P. Mc Carthy, Director, Northeast Operations, Boston

From: G.T. Case, Director, I.G.O. HQ, Greenglade, MD.

Re: Luis Jesús Ortiz

Get me a complete report on the above-named subject. I want anything and everything you can get on him. Pay special attention to anything usable to exert pressure on the subject. He is a potential source of trouble to the Organization. I want this report yesterday!

Case

Memo

Feb. 20

To: G.T. Case, Director, I.G.O. HQ, Greenglade, MD.

From: A.P. McCarthy, Director, Northeast Operations, Boston

59

Re: Luis Jesús Ortiz

As per your order, an in-depth study was done on the above-named subject. I used a team of three agents for surveillance, plus our own agent, Professor G.B. Lehrer (see his persfile).

Lehrer teaches in the physics department at M.I.T. and, by a stroke of luck, is Luis Ortiz' faculty adviser. He also has the trust and confidence of the subject. Ortiz has been the object of Lehrer's scrutiny for some time, in consequence of the incident covered in Lehrer's report which accompanies this memo. I don't know how long this report of Lehrer's has been languishing in the files. As it was low priority at the time, I'd say this report of his is over six months old. The report itself is undated. (Lehrer is sometimes a bit vague. A scientific genius, but vague nonetheless.)

My surveillance team turned up nothing but the fact that the subject cannot be successfully shadowed. On two occasions, he left his apartment in Cambridge, turned a corner, and shook off an experienced field operative. Once, he doubled back, accosted his "shadow" from behind, and demanded to know the reason he was being followed! Are you sure this kid is an amateur? He has uncanny skill in motion and some sort of sixth sense when he's being watched that allows him to shake anyone. I know; I tried it myself.

And the little monster never seems to sleep. His apartment window is visible from the street. Lights burn at all hours, and he's seen passing by the window and heard moving about on our planted listening equipment. The only places he goes are his apartment,

60

the school, and once in a while to a movie at the Cambridge Art Theater. Oh yes, once a day, at about 11:00 P.M., he goes to the school gym. He works out on the squash court. My people can't follow him into the court itself; they'd be seen. But he's in there. We can hear the ball making contact with the walls of the squash court.

I checked this out, as there was a puzzling element. The subject doesn't seem to own a squash racket. It turns out that Professor Lehrer's report covers this very detail. I later planted a camera at the squash court. What Lehrer says is so.

Report

To: A.P. Mc Carthy, Director, Northeast Operations, Boston

From: Gregory Lehrer, Field Operative code name: Dome

Re: Luis Jesús Ortiz

In keeping with I.G.O. directive # R-643-A (recruiting new candidates), I wish to draw your attention to the talents of the above-named subject. Though the subject is a minor child, I'd suggest keeping an eye on him for I.G.O. recruitment.

I am aware of the impropriety of suggesting that a sixteen-year-old boy be recruited. But this is no ordinary adolescent. I knew of his outstanding scholastic record, of course. There are few boys his age doing graduate work at this institution. And though precocity in scholastic matters isn't rare (we've had a number of very young students as part of our gifted children's program), when that precocity is combined with an uncanny athletic talent, Luis Ortiz deserves mention.

Three months ago, I was approached by a fellow faculty member. He supervises athletics for our younger talents, as obviously their age and size prevents their participating in most college-level athletics. This faculty member, Mr. Alfred Metzger, wanted some mathematical information.

While I'm sure Mr. Metzger is an excellent athletic coach, his concepts of science are somewhat sketchy. He began by asking me about rebound rates of rubber balls; moments of force. I finally stopped him and asked specifically what he wanted. Instead of explaining, he asked me to meet him at the school's squash court that night at eleven o'clock.

At the gym, we met with young Ortiz. He was already togged out in his gym shorts, top, and sneakers. As I am Luis' faculty adviser, introductions were unnecessary. As we walked toward the room that contains the squash court, Metzger said to me, "A while back, Lou here came to my office. He wanted to use the squash court late at night. When I asked him why, he told me that he was working out there. I asked him why so late at night."

"Probably because any partner he'd have during regular hours would be too mature physically. He wouldn't stand a chance in a game with a physical adult," I suggested.

"Nothing like it," replied Metzger. He motioned to

Ortiz to enter the court. We took the stairway to the upper gallery that allows spectators to watch the squash games. "He doesn't play squash on the court," Metzger continued as we entered the gallery.

I looked down on the court and must admit that young Ortiz looked very small, surrounded by the concrete walls. But he carried no racket. He had instead a half dozen or more brightly colored balls, each smaller than a handball.

"Those things are called Super Balls," Metzger explained. "They bounce and rebound like nothing you've ever seen."

I watched as Ortiz gently lobbed one of the spheres at the wall in front of him. Once I saw the ball rebound, I knew what Metzger meant. These balls are made in San Gabriel, California, by the same firm that makes the flying saucer toy called a *Frisbee.* My son and I often play with one in our front yard. They're made from a number of rubber compounds, primarily petro-chemical rubbers like the Butyl series. They are also molded under tremendous pressure. The result is a rebound rate of 85 percent or better.

If your physics are sketchy, Mr. Director, here's what that rebound percentage means. The Super Ball rebounds with 85 percent of the energy used to propel it. By comparison, a well-hit tennis ball rebounds at 50 percent and loses 50 percent of the energy with each successive bounce. A teen-ager with a good throw can have a Super Ball rebounding at speeds up to eighty miles per hour! The simple act of bouncing one of these high-density balls against a squash court wall and catching it on the rebound requires quick reflexes. Once this is understood, my report takes on a different aspect.

Down on the court, Ortiz hurled one of these at the wall in front of him. It whizzed back, narrowly missing him, as he let it pass over his shoulder. In the same motion, he threw another ball against the wall to his right. By this time, the first ball he threw was returning from bouncing against the wall behind him.

With a casual, almost balletic grace, he reached up and tapped the ball as it flew by him overhead. The ball continued and rebounded as fast as before. At this point, Ortiz threw another at the wall to his left, while performing the tapping maneuver on the second ball.

One by one, while still keeping the other balls bouncing, Ortiz added more and more of these spheres to his little game. Finally, he had no less than *eight* of these objects whizzing about the squash court, all at speeds I'd estimate at around eighty miles per hour!

As to Ortiz, he seemed to exert himself minimally. He moved among the pattern of hurtling rubber balls like a dancer. Each time one of the spheres slowed down, he'd perform the tapping motion I described earlier. At this point, Metzger grabbed at my arm and said, "See what I mean? Isn't that impossible, what he's doing? He's got eight of those Super Balls bouncing off of five surfaces—four walls and the floor. He not only keeps 'em all going, but he never gets hit by one, either!"

"If it were impossible, Mr. Metzger," I replied, "he wouldn't be doing it. Believe your eyes, sir."

"But I figured it out," insisted Metzger. "With each ball taking a path of rebound same as it's thrown, and there being eight of them for five surfaces, he *has* to get hit by one. The paths crisscross every square foot of the court!"

"You're not dealing with plane geometry here, Mr. Metzger," I explained patiently. "The surface of the Super Ball has a very high friction coefficient. If the ball is spinning when it hits, it won't bounce back at the same angle at which it's thrown."

"You mean the 'English' on the balls?" asked Metzger. "My goodness, that's even tougher to figure!"

"For you perhaps," I said dryly. "Young Ortiz has no trouble at all with the problem."

"But mathematically, it can't be done," my companion insisted.

"Use your eyes, Metzger," I snapped, losing patience. "He can do it."

I made my excuses to Metzger and left hurriedly. I wanted to check some figures. I obtained the dimensions of the court, the weight and size of Ortiz, the length of his arms (for reach), the exact friction coefficient of the Super Ball, its exact chemical make-up, and weight. I tested for resilience of the wood floor in the squash court later that night. I collected all the facts I could, then sat down and waited for my access time to the main computer, at 6:00 A.M.

It took an hour to simply set up the question for the computer, so many variables were involved. Which is why I'm not satisfied with the answer I got. The computer says that what Ortiz did is impossible too! I must have got some figures wrong. But I've checked and re-checked.

In summary, Luis Ortiz has the most remarkable set of physical and mental reflexes I've heard of. This boy could be put in a room the size of a squash court and surrounded by eight athletes with excellent responses, and try as they might, none of them could so much as lay a finger on the boy, if he did not wish to be touched. I feel the combination of his extraordinary intellect and superb physical condition warrant recruitment as soon as he is of age.

Lehrer

And that's all we have on Luis Ortiz, Mr. Case. Do you wish the surveillance continued? I have three men on him, for all the good it seems to do. Awaiting further instructions.

McCarthy

Memo

To: A.P. McCarthy, Director, Northeast Operations, Boston

From: G.T. Case, Director, I.G.O. HQ, Greenglade, MD.

Re: Luis Ortiz

Continue surveillance as best you can. If you can't keep tabs on this kid, I'll find someone within the Organization who can. I want daily reports. If the subject makes any motion to leave town, pick him up.

Case

Martin Grossman

Just a coincidence that I saw it. It must be a morbid streak in my make-up. Whenever there's a disaster, I have to read the casualty lists. And there it was: J.B. ORTIZ OF EAST HAMPTON, LONG ISLAND. Poor Johnny Ortiz.

Was it an accident? I wish I knew. If what Ortiz suspected is so, it wouldn't be hard for a paranormal adept to bring down an airplane. Especially during landing procedure. Myra says that she feels wrong vibrations about the whole Ianos Iorga movement. Someone inside the YPI Church is practicing mind control of a very sophisticated sort. Maybe Iorga himself, maybe someone with access to Iorga's people.

I laid it all out on paper. That helps me sometimes when I can see a problem diagramed. It gives me an overview.

1. We may be dealing with an organism like that we encountered during the Eddie Rodriguez affair. Or as the I.G.O. would call it, NIETZSCHE.

2. NIETZSCHE was a combination of the mentalities of Eddie Rodriguez, a Puerto Rican ghetto child, and a creature from our own future history. This creature, which is pure mental energy, took up residence in Rodriguez' mind and body at a time when the boy was close to death from meningitis. Using its tremendous mental powers, the creature expanded Rodriguez' mental capacity, which was already considerable. It

67

even used the regenerative powers of the body to make Rodriguez a perfect physical specimen. The result was a mental and physical super-being.

3. The new Eddie Rodriguez was not only a super-genius, he was a paranormal adept. He was telepathic, could project whatever image of himself he so desired, and could predict the future on a short-term basis. Once he had been to a location anywhere on earth and memorized its coordinates, he could even project himself there!

4. Rodriguez, by occupying the mind and body of Johnny Ortiz, gained entry to the I.G.O. headquarters at Greenglade, Maryland. He then abandoned Ortiz' body and entered the master computer for Western defense, an acre-square, talking, self-programming monster called ODIN. Unfortunately, while he left his own body in a trance-like, near-dead state, it was found and an autopsy performed. He had no place else to go.

5. Rodriguez went mad. Paranoid psychotic. He attempted to rule the world and nearly succeeded. But Rodriguez trusted Myra, his psychiatrist, when he was a teen-ager. He made her telepathic to act as his liaison. It was his undoing. Acting with Darryl Henskey, who was then head of I.G.O., they hatched a plot. They activated a safety device on the ODIN controls that caused it to self-destruct. In theory, Rodriguez/NIETZS-CHE died with it.

6. Myra, who was told by Rodriguez/NIETZSCHE of his true nature, explained to us that Eddie was not an isolated case. She said that some of the greatest and most infamous men in history have been hybrids mentally. She also said that the degree of success when the two personalities (one from the future and one from

68

today) mixed determined the kind of person you'd end up with. It explained all sorts of genius: Hitler and Ghandi, Attila and Aquinas. Partial blends often resulted in what was taken for demonic possession, even the werewolf/vampire tales. What's important to remember is that NIETZSCHE wasn't the only being like this.

Conclusions:

(A) We are dealing with a being of this sort. Either Rodriguez/NIETZSCHE somehow escaped before the computer blew, or we have another being from the future to deal with.

(B) There is an excellent chance that the being in question is somewhere inside the Ianos Iorga-YPI Church. He is controlling the organization and is looking to gather power—both temporal and financial as well as spiritual.

(C) We don't stand a chance of fighting him. It was only a fluke chance that saved the world from holocaust last time a creature like this showed up. What to do?

I'm going to present all this to Myra.

Luis Ortiz

I hope fatso got the message okay. The look on his face when I told him I knew what his story really was! What a turkey. And that's what's supposed to be defending the United States against foreign enemies? No wonder we're in such bad shape. That guy shouldn't be in a position of power. He's a top-flight, second-rate mind. He should work for someone, not be the boss.

I had a hunch there was something really wrong when Johnny called me from New York. And my hunches have a way of coming to pass. I should have known it was going sour from that dream I had just before Johnny died on the plane.

Johnny was in uniform, like a W.W. II pilot. He was being ordered to fly a mission by a colonel I didn't recognize. Johnny got into the plane, and then the whole thing went up in a big explosion of flames. The stupid colonel stood there watching it all happen. Then he just walked away. Didn't run to the wreckage or even try to help.

I should trust my dreams more. I recognize that colonel now. It was George T. Case. If it turns out that Johnny died because of that man's stupidity . . .

George Case

Stupid! I've been the prize dummy of the century. And Ortiz stumbled on it. I should have seen it right away. Everyone connected with Iorga recites like a parrot: *Brother Ianos is a saint.* When I was tracking down NIETZSCHE, everyone recited the same tale about Eddie Rodriguez. All the world loved him. He was a bright, intelligent, respectful, wonderful kid. To *everybody.* Nobody bats a thousand. That alone should have tipped me. Any time Rodriguez used a person, he left a post-hypnotic suggestion that Eddie was the greatest guy in the world. Just like Iorga.

Except Iorga is going NIETZSCHE one better. The world is calling him a saint, no less. If he's a saint, I'm the Holy Trinity. I've got to talk to someone about this. The someone is Darryl Henskey. Got to book a flight to Maine. Also got to check with his doctor to see if he can be interviewed. The stroke that retired him made him a basket case. His mind is okay. He has trouble getting his body to work. And speak and walk. Brrr. If it ever happens to me, I hope it kills me outright. I couldn't take spending the rest of my life in a wheelchair and being fed by hand.

Denver Register

Iorga Heals Crippled Child at Rally outside the City

February 26—At a rally to greet Ianos Iorga, the famed Rumanian holy man who is making what he calls a coast-to-coast pilgrimage, brought a crowd of over twenty thousand to near hysteria when he allegedly cured young Charles Linnet of Denver. Linnet, a cripple from a severe automobile accident that broke his spinal column and left him a paraplegic, got up from his wheelchair and took a number of steps, eyewitnesses report.

The "cure" was effected in full sight of the crowd, which included several important members of the Denver medical community. To a man, all the doctors present confirm that the Linnet boy did walk. However, none would comment on the case further without having seen X-rays and other medical history on young Linnet.

Brother Ianos will be in Denver for one more day. He will then continue his three-thousand-mile walk which is to culminate in a giant rally at Yankee Stadium in New York.

Linda Maxwell

Wonder what old sweaty palms wants? I try to stay away from Case's office as much as possible since that last interview I had with him. The old goat. He's got to be fifty-five if he's a day. And there he is looking me over like I was a dessert, and he'd just finished dinner. Case gives me the creeps. I felt it was just a matter of time before he came on to me. What do you do when the head of the Organization makes a pass? Receive gracefully? Not this kid! I've got a grade-six clearance, and my proficiency reports are in the top ten for the Organization. If he makes one move, I walk. On the Organization, on Washington, and all the phonies I've met here. Get me back to New York!

George Case

As I recall Maxwell is a beautiful kid. She must have thought I was some kind of nut the way I stared at her. But she is the image of my sister Margaret. At the same age, of course. The important thing is that she looks a

72

good deal younger than twenty-two. She could pass for being in her late teens easily. And that's the age we need. The problem is explaining the mission to her without telling her too much.

Her file says she's a grade-six. Cleared through MOST SECRET. Specialty is languages. Can fly a helicopter, also light plane, two-engine license. Not bad . . . almost said not bad for a woman. Got to watch that. E.R.A. is everywhere. But I do have reservations about sending her in to infiltrate the YPI movement. Silly, I guess. Just because she's a woman and looks like my dead sister. She's a qualified operative. And a very good one, from her record.

Martin Grossman

Myra doesn't want to do anything. I told her that I wanted to bring the Ortiz matter before the I.G.O. She says that if anything irregular did take place in the jet crash at Dulles, the I.G.O. would find it out soon enough. Mostly, I think Myra wants no part of the I.G.O. She has an understandably low opinion of any Secret Police agency. She knew the Gestapo firsthand when she was a little girl in W.W. II—and somehow survived a death camp. She says that she only interfered in the NIETZSCHE affair because she felt partly responsible. But if there is another NIETZSCHE-thing around, no one's safe. I told her that her attitude was unreal. I reminded her that the inhabitants of the War-saw ghetto also stood by because it was happening to someone else. By the time they realized they had to fight, it was too late. She only replied, "This is not Poland." I'll wait her out.

Rafael Guzman

Heard from Eddie. He took a chance sending me all that cash in the envelope. I hear some of the temporary guys at the post office are always on the lookout for envelopes that feel like there's cash in 'em. I guess he knows that I get my mail right from the mailman at the store. Around this neighborhood, a check or money in the mail ain't safe. Junkies and *sinvergüenzas* always ripping off the mailboxes.

He wants me to rent a place for him in Brooklyn! I don't even know the neighborhood he talks about. Where the hell is Sheepshead Bay? Not that I care. If Eddie told me to go to Russia, I'd go. I already picked up the *Times.* They got a lotta places for rent in the paper. If you want to spend that kind of coin on a place to live. Some of these places in Sheepshead Bay go for heavy bread. But Eddie sent me plenty. I gotta remember the name to use too. Ortiz. Where does he think these things up from?

Linda Maxwell

What a relief. It was an assignment. And a real one! This is what I joined I.G.O. for. I was beginning to think that all I'd ever get was a glorified clerical post. Around here, they seem to think that intelligence work is a man's game. They forget that women are the best at it. I've been concealing the fact that I'm an intelligent person from men most of my life.

George Case

Henskey is dead. A fire swept through his place in Maine. Killed him and his nurse. They were cut off by the heavy snow. By the time the fire equipment got to the place, it was ashes. This doesn't smell right. Henskey, of course, didn't smoke. The nurse wouldn't; it was bad for Henskey. The fire report says a mattress fire. Henskey's bed. The whole place burned in minutes. No arson. That's what the local fire laddies say. I'm going to send up my own crew to check it out.

Memo

Mar. 1

To: G.T. Case, Director, I.G.O. HQ, Greenglade, MD.

From: Field Agent L. Maxwell

Re: Ianos Iorga and YPI Church

I have been approached by proselytizers from the YPI. I hadn't been in Greenwich Village in New York City for two days when I was sounded on a street corner. I agreed to go to the meeting scheduled for this coming Friday. I did fill out their preliminary questionnaire, using the cover identity provided. I just hope that this Gloria Steinberg stays in Europe, or wherever she is with her parents. By the way, the apartment on lower Fifth Avenue is gorgeous. Not so my Organization "parents" who seem to have gotten their undercover training from a mail order course in "How to Be a Detective." Really, was this the best we had? Will report after the Friday prayer meeting.

Maxwell

Memo

Mar. 1

To: Secretary of State

From: G.T. Case, Director, I.G.O. HQ, Greenglade, MD.

Re: Ianos Iorga and YPI Church (preliminary report)

Dear Mr. Secretary:

Your suspicions may have been well founded. In pursuing our investigation of the YPI Church, more and more irregularities are arising. We have a found a tenuous connection between all three deaths. The nature of this connection should be discussed privately. This office does not care to speculate in print on the more bizarre aspects.

When you have time, I should like an appointment to talk this over more fully. I realize, sir, that you have a heavy schedule and are due to make another Mid East swing. If possible, I would like to see you before then.

Sincerely,

Case

Linda Maxwell

I never realized that it was a conspiracy. The I.G.O., the government, they're all in on it. They want to keep Brother Ianos from spreading the truth. I never would have known. But last night, I met Brother Ianos!

I thought he was still in Colorado, but Sister Evelyn tells me that he often slips away. When I asked how, she gave me the answer I was beginning to expect: "He can be in all places at all times."

Brother Ianos only spoke to me for a second. In that moment, I knew he was The Second Coming. I confessed all my sins to Him. I felt so unworthy for having plotted against Him. I told him everything. My I.G.O. background, the assignment to infiltrate the YPI Church. If I had expected anger and rejection, I was wrong. This beautiful person only took my hand and said, "It's all right, Linda. I knew all along. I love you, and Jesus loves you."

He forgave me on the spot! And he isn't asking me to work against the I.G.O., either. He only said, "Go forth and sin no more. Spread the Word of God." And that is just what I shall do. Sister Evelyn has given me some pamphlets. And an airline ticket to Kansas City. By tomorrow, I will be there, spreading the Word.

Memo

Mar. 1

To: G.T. Case, Director, I.G.O. HQ, Greenglade, MD.

From: Records

Re: Crank mail

The attached postal card came in today's mail. Checked it for ink type, point of purchase, pen used (it's in longhand), fingerprints, trace chemicals. All negative. The card itself is a standard view of New York City skyline. There are approximately 250,000 in circulation at over 5,000 outlets in the metropolitan area. In short, untraceable. The card is addressed to you and is cryptic. Checked it through Cipher Division, and it employs no cipher known to this agency. It would appear to be a crank mail piece.

Specimen

GEORGE T. CASE
INTERNATIONAL INFORMATION
    GATHERING ORGANIZATION
GREENGLADE, MD.

Dear Stinky,
 An amateur try, at best.
I am lonely, though. Send
me another agent when
you get the time.

George Case

It may be the break I've been looking for! Maybe his overconfidence is his weak point. Now that I know it's NIETZSCHE, I can plan. At least I know what I'm dealing with. I should have guessed when he killed Henskey. Which means that Myra Sokolow and Martin Grossman are in deadly danger. This is more than Rodriguez returned from the grave. He's after revenge too!

I've set up a Priority Ten emergency status for all units. Security at HQ is going to be near-impossible. NIETZSCHE could be anyone walking around the building. He even fooled ODIN the last time. At least that mess can't be repeated. We have it set up now that no central point can patch into our computer systems again. Ever.

But one by one, he's killing everyone responsible for bringing him down the last time. Henskey's dead. So is Ortiz. That leaves only Sokolow, Grossman, and me. I've got a million plans in my head, but all of them seem useless. They're based on security. And security is based on silence. NIETZSCHE can read minds. There goes any kind of security. My case ace is going to be Grossman and Sokolow. They've dealt with Rodriguez before.

They may have ideas. Unless Rodriguez has already gotten to them too! This is impossible. I can't trust anyone. Except me.

Martin Grossman

It's like some grisly *déjà vu* experience. Here I am on a military aircraft with Myra bound for Greenglade. Case pulled some strings and activated my I.G.O. agent/adviser status. I'm under orders. Oddly enough, Myra came without any fuss. I wish that I could read her thoughts as easily as she reads mine. All I can pick up are general feelings, emotions. Myra says what I have is a good basic empathic sense. It's akin to telepathy, but works at a lower level. I wish . . . well, I wish a lot of things. But nothing will be resolved until we have a conference with Case. How I do wish Henskey were still alive. That was a shock too. Funny. Myra wouldn't even consider seeing anyone from I.G.O. until she learned of Henskey's death.

Kansas City Post

Another YPI Death?

OVERLAND PARK, March 2—An automobile driven by one of the many followers of Rumanian holy man, Ianos Iorga, plunged from the bluffs overlooking the river.

The driver was positively identified as Gloria Steinberg of New York City. Her parents, vacationing in Europe, were notified and declined comment to our Paris Bureau. YPI spokesmen voiced no opinion, other than regret over the tragic accident. Iorga is due to arrive in Kansas City this Tuesday on his Long Walk to New York.

Martin Grossman

At least I understand now. When we were getting off the plane, she finally broke her silence. Said she'd been thinking things out. An amazing woman. Here I'd been racking my brain, trying to think up some sort of defense against Eddie Rodriguez. I couldn't find any. But Myra, as our street kids in the assistance program say, is something else.

We were traveling by I.G.O. limo to the Greenglade complex. Myra began to communicate with me telepathically.

"If Case has any sense," she said, "he'll put us in isolation and interview us by closed-circuit TV. That way, if Eddie has reached either of us, we won't be inside the I.G.O. complex. He knows that the *psi* powers Eddie possesses don't work over electronic transmission."

"And once he clears us, we can enter. Clever," I said.

"No," said Myra. "Elementary and easily bypassed. All Eddie would have to do is lie convincingly to Case. Even going through our dossiers and asking trick questions can't do it. Eddie would have complete access to any information our minds and memories possessed."

"Then what defense would be effective?" I asked.

"There is only one," she replied. "And that defense is Myra Sokolow."

"You alone?"

"Exactly. Eddie, whether in person or controlling someone, gives off an aura of *psi* power. I pick up the vibrations immediately. It's as though he were a radio transmitting station, and I were a constantly operating receiver. If Eddie is near, I'll sense him."

"Then the Greenglade complex *can* be defended?"

"Yes. But if I tell this to Case, I'll be confined here until such time as Eddie is apprehended or stopped. I will not be a live-in watchdog to protect the files and equipment for an organization that I feel shouldn't exist. I.G.O. is a Secret Police agency. I will not risk my life and sanity to defend it."

"But surely, Myra, you see the gravity of the situation. The threat that Eddie poses to us all."

"I do. That is the one reason I am here. But I must exercise caution. You see, Martin, Darryl Henskey was the only man in I.G.O. that knew I was telepathic. This man Case never knew how Henskey and I worked to destroy the ODIN computer. He still believes that Henskey worked out the computer/destruct mechanism on his own."

"But that's unlike Henskey," I protested. "He would have put it all into a report to the President."

"I think not, for two reasons," Myra said. "First, if he had, I never would have been allowed to leave Greenglade. I would have become I.G.O.'s new secret weapon. Interrogating captives, monitoring conferences telepathically. And that did not happen. The second reason is that Henskey owed me my privacy and peace in return for my showing him how to defeat Eddie Rodriguez."

"You know all this for sure?"

"Yes. I read it in his mind when he released us. I don't believe he would have been comfortable with a telepath on his staff. As you know, with a telepath, secrecy is impossible. And you do know these Gestapo types love their little plots and conspiracies. I would have been an embarrassment to him. No, he never filed his report, Martin."

"Then how will you deal with Case?" I asked.

"The very problem I have been wrestling with since Johnny Ortiz came to see us. I know a great deal of how we can try to fight Eddie Rodriguez. But to use my information, I must admit to Case that I am a telepath. That is where you come in, Martin."

"I? What in the world can I do? You've already said that only you can help."

"You and I know that. Case doesn't. Do you recall when you were trying to build a mechanical detector for *psi* impulses?"

"That was before I found out from you and Eddie that *psi* impulses are a different form of energy. There's no machine in the world that can pick it up."

"Again, Case does not know this. Once he clears us through his useless remote TV interview, you will tell him that you can build a *psi* detector. He will requisition any materials you need. Order a complicated set of parts. The more expensive the better. Governments believe that a weapon is only effective if it costs a great deal. Then tell him that we can operate it. Once he believes his precious headquarters are safe from infiltration, he will relax enough to allow us some freedom of motion. If we are to be of any use at all against Eddie, we must be able to come and go when we need to. Can you do as I ask?"

"Yes, I think so. Offhand, I can think of two or three of my past attempts that were impressive financially. Naturally, none of them worked. I'll add another circuit or two. No one will know."

"We're approaching the Greenglade complex now," said Myra. "Be sure to communicate vocally with me. Don't use telepathy unless I give you a sign. Case may be a policeman, but he is far from stupid."

Text of Remote TV Interview, Mar. 3

Subjects Grossman and Sokolow were screened by remote TV interrogation before being admitted to Greenglade. Interrogation was conducted by Organization Director George T. Case, after preliminary visual identification. (Both subjects are known to G.T. Case. Grossman is an agent/adviser. See his persfile. Code designation: WALLFLOWER. Sokolow is a civilian who assisted us on the NIETZSCHE affair two years ago. See NIETZSCHE file.)

CASE: Good evening, doctors. Dr. Sokolow, do you remember me?

SOK.: Yes, Mr. Case, I do.

CASE: Dr. Grossman. Who recruited you for I.G.O.?

GROSS.: Darryl Henskey. In 1970.

CASE: To both of you: Have you ever known me by any other name?

SOK.: Yes. Do you wish that name repeated?

CASE: It doesn't please me, but yes, I do.

SOK.: The name is Stinky.

GROSS.: Mr. Case, this interview is useless, if you'll permit me to say so. NIETZSCHE would know all the same information. I have been working on an electronic device that may be able to protect headquarters from infiltration. Do you wish to discuss it under these circumstances?

CASE: No. I'll allow you in. I didn't think this would work, anyhow.

George Case

What a relief! Bless Grossman. I should have remembered that he'd been working on a device like this for years. Can't say I understand it, but as Grossman explains it, it's like a radar for *psi* powers. Anytime there's a *thing* like NIETZSCHE nearby, the needle on the dial swings into the red. It has graduated scales. Seems everyone, even I, can possess a certain amount of *psi* ability. He showed me my own pattern. Very low reading compared to him and Sokolow. Grossman says that's because they have both been working at developing their own *psi* powers for treating patients. However, neither of them can make it swing to red. Grossman says that if a being as powerful as NIETZSCHE comes anywhere near, the needle will wrap itself around the pin.

The device is simple enough to assemble. It's even cheap to make except for one detail. The protective case has to be made of solid gold! The model that Grossman assembled today used lead shielding, but Grossman says that it's only 75 percent effective this way. Accounting is going to go through the ceiling.

We'll need devices at every entrance to the complex. That will mean over forty of them. And I can't forget the trash collection loading dock, either. For a number of reasons. I still recall when we were all Rodriguez' prisoners here at Greenglade. I tried to sneak out through the garbage collection. He caught me at it. For two weeks everybody had to call me Stinky. NIETZSCHE's orders. It was embarrassing, but it made a good password when clearing Sokolow and Grossman.

Rafael Guzman

I got the place Eddie wanted. It's in Sheepshead Bay right near the water, just like he said. I used the name Ortiz, like I was supposed to. They was all set to give me the chill at that real estate office until they saw the color of the money. What Eddie always said is right. If you're a *Latino* and poor, the world craps on you. Soon as you got money, all of a sudden, you're everyone's *hermano*. That dude at King's Realty couldn't do enough for me when he seen the roll of hundreds.

Trouble is, now I don't know who to give the key to the Brooklyn place to. I'm sure I'll hear from Eddie again, though. He'll let me know.

St. Louis City Star

Iorga's Long Walk at Halfway Mark in St. Louis

February 28—Rumanian holy man Ianos Iorga has reached the midpoint in his self-styled pilgrimage to New York City.

Iorga has been walking and preaching his way across the country in what he describes as an effort to revive religion in the United States. He has been greeted by adoring crowds every step of the way. A good percentage of the curious and faithful have followed him on his walk each stop he makes.

At present, the entourage in Iorga's wake make up a column of marching humanity over two miles long. Authorities here, fearful of riots and potential health hazards accompanying a group of this size, denied Iorga a parade permit, thereby blocking his entrance into St. Louis. Undaunted, Iorga camped just outside the city limit.

Western Union Telegram

MARCH 2

G.T. CASE DIRECTOR I.G.O. HEADQUARTERS GREEN-GLADE MD

WHERE'S MY REPORT? OR DO I SING MY SONG TO THE POST?

LUIS ORTIZ

George Case

That's all I needed. I can't play games with this kid. I'm going to order him picked up and brought down here. I've got enough on my plate without worrying about some smartass punk spilling his guts to the newspapers. *The Post* would love to get their hands on this.

Memo

From: G.T. Case, Director, I.G.O. HQ, Greenglade, MD.

To: A.P. McCarthy, Director, Northeast Operations, Boston

Re: Luis Ortiz

March 2

Don't be put off by his age. Ortiz comprises a threat to international security. Pick him up. I want him at Maryland HQ within the next twelve hours. He is to be kept absolutely incommunicado. Don't worry about loose ends. Legal dept. will pick up the pieces if necessary. Just get me that kid! USE MILITARY TRANSPORT ONLY.

Case

Martin Grossman

It's amazing! I'm still reeling from the force of his power. This is the chance of a lifetime. Myra says the boy doesn't even know what has happened to him. But to be able to study this phenomenon up close and without danger. It's enough to make me forget the threat that Rodriguez poses as he gets closer and closer to New York.

Memo

Mar. 3

To: The President of the United States

From: Secretary of State

Re: Ianos Iorga and the YPI Church

Dear Mr. President:

Attached are transcripts, files, and reports. I draw your attention to the transcript of the interview with Director Case, Drs. Sokolow and Grossman, and subject Luis Ortiz. The interview came about by accident.

By order of Director Case, the boy Ortiz was detained at our Greenglade installation. Case felt young Ortiz comprised a security threat in the new NIETZS-CHE affair. Subject was being held incommunicado and with military escort, was being led to a detention apartment in one of Greenglade's above-ground levels. As Ortiz and his escort passed Case, Grossman, and Sokolow in a public corridor, Sokolow suddenly cried out and collapsed in a dead faint. She was brought immediately to the infirmary wing. When she regained consciousness, she urgently requested the interview transcribed below. The interview was conducted under Priority Ten (10) security at one of the Greenglade interrogation areas. Transcript follows.

Transcript: Interrogation, Luis Ortiz Session One (xb: 12. p. 6)

Personnel present: Director G.T. Case, Drs. M. Sokolow, M. Grossman

Security clearance: PRIORITY TEN (10)

Location: Interrogation Area C

CASE: Are you certain that you're up to this, Dr. Sokolow?

SOK.: I think so.

CASE: I can't risk your health, doctor. You're too important.

SOK.: I find your concern for my health touching, Mr. Case. No, you may bring the boy in at any time.

CASE: You have read our file on him?

SOK.: Yes, and it's very interesting as far as it goes. I need much more, if my suspicions are correct.

CASE: What is it you suspect?

SOK.: I'll tell you more when I know more. There is no point in, uh, getting ahead of ourselves.

CASE: (into intercom) Sergeant, bring in the Ortiz boy. *(Door open and close)*

ORTIZ: What's this all about, Case? I know you threatened me with arrest. I've already left a letter with a friend in case I was picked up. By now, my father is on the horn with the best lawyers in the country. This isn't Russia, you know.

CASE: I know about the letter. I have it here. Your Professor Lehrer is one of my agents. So if you're waiting for the cavalry to arrive, you'll have a long wait.

ORTIZ: Oh, great. Maybe this is Russia after all.

CASE: I'd like you to meet Drs. Myra Sokolow and Martin Grossman, Luis.

ORTIZ: Who are they, more of your stooges?

SOK.: No, we are not, Luis. We were friends of your brother, Johnny.

ORTIZ: And you just happen to be hanging around here for laughs. Please, lady, don't insult my intelligence.

SOK.: Far from it, Luis. I respect your intelligence immensely. It's the reason I requested this interview.

ORTIZ: You mean that you're the real boss? It figures. I thought that Case here was someone's stooge. I can't see a second-rate mind like his in charge of a setup like this.

92

SOK.: (laughing) No, no. The last thing on earth I would want is to be a part of an agency like this. What has happened is an international emergency, which I am sure concerns you little. But what you *will* be interested in is the fact that we have discovered your brother's murderer. And it's all wrapped up in this charade of security we have found ourselves in. Will you answer some questions for me, Luis?

ORTIZ: It depends on what they are. Ask ahead. If you come to some I don't like, you'll know it.

SOK.: Have you had any childhood illnesses, Luis?

ORTIZ: Not a one. I've had shots for all childhood diseases. Why?

SOK.: Have you ever had an injury that rendered you unconscious for any length of time?

ORTIZ: Never.

SOK.: How are your teeth? Any dental work?

ORTIZ: My teeth are perfect. Never had a cavity in my life. We fluoridize the water in my home town. Listen, what's this about? If you want my medical history, it's on file at M.I.T. and with my family doctor in East Hampton.

CASE: It's been sent for. It hasn't arrived yet.

SOK.: Please, Mr. Case, you promised me free access to this young man.

CASE: Sorry, doctor. Proceed.

SOK.: Luis, how long did it take you to complete your basic education?

ORTIZ: It's still going on. I'm studying for my doctorate in physics at M.I.T. now.

SOK.: And you are presently sixteen years of age?

ORTIZ: I'll be seventeen in October.

SOK.: One more thing. I recall from what your

brother Johnny told me, that your mother died when you were born. Is this true?

ORTIZ: Yes. It was an auto accident. I was six weeks premature. I was in an incubator for a time. But I'm fine now. Have been all my life.

SOK.: Thank you so much, Luis. That's all I need, Mr. Case. Mr. Ortiz can leave now.

CASE: (into intercom) Sergeant, you may take Mr. Ortiz to his apartment. *(Background noises. Door open and close)*

CASE: Well?

GROS.: Did you see the needle? It's way off the scale.

CASE: If I'd have had a gun, I'd have killed him on the spot.

SOK.: I believe you would have, Mr. Case. And that's a shame. You would have lost the only chance you have to stand up to Eddie Rodriguez.

CASE: Am I going nuts? Are you telling me that the boy we just talked to *isn't* Eddie Rodriguez? Is this *psi* gizmo wrong?

SOK.: It's working as well as it ever did. But Luis Ortiz is *not* Eddie Rodriguez, nor is he being controlled by him.

CASE: My God! You mean to tell me that Ortiz is . . .

SOK.: Precisely. He is another, different creature. And extremely powerful. Perhaps even stronger than Eddie. I can't tell. He seems unaware of his own capabilities. I must speak with him. Alone and with no one listening in. Can that be arranged?

CASE: I suppose.

SOK.: Good. Give him a day to rest up. I'd like to see him tomorrow.

CASE: You've got it, lady. And I hope you're right.
SOK.: So do I, Mr. Case. So do I.

END TRANSCRIPT

Martin Grossman

Myra and I were on our way to Case's office when it happened. Luis Ortiz was being led past us, a marine guard at his elbow. From what Myra tells me, when she is in public places, she scans the crowds. Sometimes, she picks up *psi* vibrations from unlikely sources. It's a process something like window-shopping. When she spots a talent source, she doesn't necessarily do anything about it; just notes it and walks on by.

As Ortiz was passing us in the corridor, Myra sent out a gentle probe, almost absent-mindedly. The response she got back from Ortiz was so strong, it stunned her! Even I felt some of it. Naturally, Myra requested an interview with the boy.

Case would have come unglued if he'd been able to hear what was really going on at that interview. The bulk of the communication between Myra and Ortiz was telepathic. I got most of Myra's end of the exchange. I guess after two years, I'm on her wave length, so to speak. It was an education. I realize now that the communication between Myra and me that I thought was so advanced is not that great. Not after being present when two full telepaths are going at it. I know now that, for two years, Myra has been "talking" with me as

95

a person with normal hearing would communicate with a deaf person. My much-prized telepathic rapport with Myra is child's play.

Myra immediately filled in Ortiz on what he may be. As the visitor from the future entered Luis' body when he was an infant (it had to be while he was in the incubator), the merging has been gradual and of great benefit to the Ortiz boy.

I find the odds against this happening staggering. And to find two such half-human, half-something-else beings in the same time period is even more unlikely.

Myra learned years ago from Rodriguez about these visitors. Centuries from now, and after a number of atomic wars, man will finally grow up and stop destroying the planet. But by then, it will almost be too late. Because of what hard radiation does to the genes, our future descendants won't look much like men do today. As an aesthetic measure, each individual projects a picture of himself to others mentally. That picture can be of his own choosing. Thus, it doesn't matter what an individual looks like. The image others see is the image he wants them to see. It's this ability that allows Rodriguez to move so freely despite surveillance. You can't tail somebody who can change his appearance at will.

This whole future society is based on *psi* power. People travel by teleportation, heavy objects are moved by psychokinesis. Communication is by telepathy. And some time way "up then," an individual will discover a way to completely separate mind and body. The entire society is going to merge into one great group consciousness. Well, not quite. As Rodriguez told Myra, certain individuals are unable to merge with the others and leave the earth for good.

These are the misfits and congenital unfits. They are the wards of this future society, much as our society cares for the brain-damaged, feeble-minded, and insane. Rather than leave these misfits to fend for themselves, they are sent backwards in time. To periods where their limited abilities will allow them to do well.

It's frightening to consider that the super-genius that we fear so much, Eddie Rodriguez, is a blend of himself and a creature that will one day be considered an idiot! It gives me pause. If this is an idiot we are dealing with, what must their geniuses be like? I almost hope that I never find out.

The exchange between Myra and Ortiz was humbling enough for me. It also was fast. All the information I've set down in my diary, she communicated to Ortiz in a matter of seconds. And all this going on while they were conducting a vocal conversation as well! I suppose she also told Ortiz how the visitors from the future can enter a person of this time. It requires a subject who is near to death, as Ortiz was when he was prematurely born. In Rodriguez' case, it was a childhood bout with meningitis.

In any event, Ortiz must have believed her. She asked him to test his psychokinetic power to move the needle on the *psi* detector. I nearly fell down when I saw the needle jump like that. I built the detector and I know it doesn't work!

When I asked Myra how come Ortiz went along with the story and her requests so easily, she replied, "He knew I was telling the truth, because you cannot lie telepathically. To read another's thoughts is to read only the truth. Naturally he co-operated. Then too there was his revenge motive. He's convinced now that Eddie Rodriguez was responsible for his brother's death."

"But surely," I objected, "he's no match for Rodriguez. Ortiz has just discovered that he has this power. Rodriguez has been practicing for years. It's like putting a talented amateur into the ring with a champion."

"I am no devotee of violent sports, Martin," Myra said. "However, I believe I have read of cases where a talented amateur has upset a professional champion. I also feel that we have enough time to train for this fight. I also think that basically, Ortiz may be stronger than Eddie."

"That could make him more of a threat than Rodriguez," I said. "Are we riding a tiger here?"

"I think not," Myra said. "The creature that shared Eddie Rodriguez and now, I believe, Ianos Iorga, is insane. His thoughts are not as organized or well directed as Ortiz' are. No, I don't feel Luis is a threat. At least not of the magnitude of an Eddie Rodriguez or a Ianos Iorga."

I hope she's right. The thought of something even stronger than Eddie is scary. I wonder what Luis Ortiz is making of all this?

Luis Ortiz

What a relief! All these years, I thought I was going flaky. Oh, I knew that I was "different." I never knew *how* different. And that "conversation" with Myra Sokolow! I feel like I've had my first talk with another human and that, up till now, I've been communicating with pencil and paper, the way some mutes do.

And all the things this news of Dr. Sokolow explains! She says my "hunches" are clairvoyance, that I can foretell the future at times. And that I can actually control objects by concentrating on them.

She read the report that the I.G.O. had on my Super Ball game. I can do it, she says, because I'm not actually catching the ball or touching it as it flies by me. I'm really controlling each of the eight Super Balls in flight. She also explained my insomnia. It always worried me. I mean, I don't feel tired or anything, but I've discovered I get by just fine on little or no sleep. I was afraid I'd get sick or something if I never slept. But what really knocks me out is the concept of utter, raw power.

I had to try out the power. See if I really could do all the things Dr. Sokolow says I can. It works, all right. As the guard outside my door was closest, I tried it out on him. I only hope Case hears about one of his marine guards running through the halls stark naked and singing *From the Halls of Montezuma* at the top of his lungs!

Dr. Sokolow says to enjoy it while I can. There's a lot

of work ahead. And Ianos Iorga or Eddie Rodriguez, whatever or whoever he is, is going to pay for killing Johnny. I'm going to think up something really special for Iorga/Rodriguez. Special and nasty!

Eyes Only (Priority Ten)

Mar. 3

To: The President of The United States

From: Secretary of State

Re: Ianos Iorga and YPI Church

Dear Mr. President:

Our worst suspicions have been confirmed. NIETZSCHE/Rodriguez did escape from the ODIN computer before it overloaded and blew. From what the I.G.O. can piece together, he left Greenglade in the body of Russian Foreign Minister Dimitri Gangov. It unhinged Gangov's mind. The Russkies sent him down to the Black Sea for a rest cure.

From there, I.G.O. speculates, he "hitchhiked" bodies until he found a suitable host in Ianos Iorga. The Iorga boy had just suffered a serious head injury, which left him comatose. At this point, NIETZSCHE/Rodriguez occupied Iorga's mind and body.

It would be all so simple to go after Ianos Iorga, then. Except for the fact that Iorga is currently one of the most important religious leaders in the world! He's wrapped up in the sanctuary of his church. He's protected by the Constitution.

From our own mutual experience that terrible night in the ODIN complex, we both know how ruthless and deadly NIETZSCHE/Rodriguez can be. I feel that this creature has not changed his goal of absolute world domination. He's only approaching it from a different angle this time. And we are near-powerless to stop him!

This *thing* controls the minds of over 70 percent of the children of the most powerful and influential persons in the Western Powers Bloc. If NIETZSCHE is not stopped, and soon, think of the consequences when all those kids start to inherit the power and wealth of the world. And, incidentally, start to vote.

We may have a counter weapon. Case of I.G.O. says he has something, I don't know what, that may help us fight NIETZSCHE. Case wants to stay mum until he can test out this device. I assume it's a device. I don't know what else it could be. Men and women are helpless in NIETZSCHE's presence!

George Case

For the first time in a long time, I'm not scared. I'm not looking twice at everyone, wondering if Rodriguez is riding around inside. It's that detector of Grossman's. I had some doubts, but when I saw the needle jump, I knew. I've expedited production on the detectors. We need forty of them here, and, of course, at every entrance to the White House.

101

When I told the Secretary of State how much these gizmos are going to cost per unit, I expected him to hit the ceiling. He just said, "Okay, requisition what you need." And we need something like four hundred pounds of pure gold! That's without the little bits of printed circuitry, which are gold, and some wiring, twenty feet per unit, of platinum. If I had a non-emergency budget like this, there wouldn't be a threat to this country anywhere in the world. Except for something like NIETZSCHE.

Chicago Herald

Iorga Rally in Joliet
Draws over 50,000

JOLIET, March 6—Perhaps mindful of being denied a parade permit in St. Louis, Brother Ianos Iorga is bypassing the city of Chicago on his Long Walk to New York.

A crowd of over 50,000 of the faithful turned out to hear the Rumanian holy man preach, just outside of Joliet. Iorga also made a visit to the Illinois State Penitentiary in Statesville. There he reportedly healed an inmate of blindness.

Brother Ianos is due to arrive in New York City for a super rally in Yankee Stadium sometime late in the spring.

Luis Ortiz

This is getting to be a drag. Maybe I did the wrong thing in going along with Sokolow's plans. She did give me a choice at the time, I have to admit. At that first conference, she told me that if I wanted, she would tell Case she was mistaken. That I don't have the *psi* powers she thought I did. I could have walked out right then and there; nobody would have known.

I don't think we're gaining anything with all these tests. Yeah, I know that they have to determine just what my strengths and weaknesses are. How distant from a subject I can be and still control him. If it makes a difference when the subject is willing or resists. All that.

But if anyone asks me, and nobody does, I think this whole testing procedure is one big picnic for Grossman. He has a good, if somewhat limited, mind. He also has *psi* potential. I think he could be an excellent empath. A fitting talent for a psychiatrist. It's a great feeling to hear someone say, "I know how you feel," and really mean it. But I feel like a new sort of bug an entomologist has discovered.

I'm going out tonight and catch a flick. I did it last night for the first time. It was easy. I just went along with my guard when the shift changed at 8:00 P.M. I projected an image of myself in bed and made myself invisible to the guards. Now that I've been to that art movie house in Georgetown, Myra says I can actually project myself there physically. I know I can teleport. I moved from Area A to Area D yesterday under test conditions. That was only twenty meters, though. Georgetown is five miles from here. Last night, I had to control a driver when I hitchhiked over there. It might be a kick to try. Grossman says I must be careful though. If my memorized co-ordinates are a bit off when I teleport, I could suddenly show up inside a solid wall. Or under the wheels of a truck or car. Not a happy thought.

Martin Grossman

The progress Ortiz is making causes my head to spin. Yesterday, he teleported a distance of twenty meters. Perfectly. We set up some co-ordinates for him to work from, and that was it. First try: 100 percent. I hope Myra's emotional hold on him is solid. Once Luis realizes the full scope of his capabilities, there will be no detaining him. Walls have no meaning to him. Nor do laws, individuals, societies, or covenants. In fact, the only thing that keeps him from being a monster of even greater magnitude than Eddie Rodriguez is his moral sense. I take my hat off to Renaldo Ortiz. He gave his kids a good set of values from the start. Johnny Ortiz was a fine young man. Luis is more flexible, but I believe of the same moral cloth as his older brother was. Thank God!

And on a purely selfish basis, I'm delighted with this turn of events. I never had a chance to study Rodriguez;

take measurements, inquire into the very nature of *psi* energy. This is a lifetime chance for me. I intend to make the most of it.

Luis Ortiz

The looks on their faces! I nearly peed my pants laughing. I transported myself to the movie house just fine. I memorized what seat I sat in the night before. I had the co-ordinates firmly fixed in my mind. I got there perfectly, too. It just never occurred to me that there might be someone sitting in the seat when I did. And there was. He was a big bruiser of a dude too.

He was there with his girlfriend, and they were doing some heavy making out. Right in the balcony. I materialized in his lap! Nearly busted his girlfriend's hand. I blanked myself out of their minds immediately, but not before they saw and felt me for a split second. The looks on their faces! I'm still laughing.

Then I took a good look at Washington. I hailed a cab and went across the bridge into D.C. proper. Around Dupont Circle. I should have known better. I am only sixteen, and the chicks in Boston have always found me reasonably attractive. All the gay guys cruising around there! I finally had to make myself unseen to walk a block without being accosted. I guess they figure if I'm out walking around there, I *want* to be picked up. I passed out of the Gaysville section in a few blocks. Got more into a black neighborhood. It was a shock. Big sections looked like they'd been bombed out. There wasn't a soul walking. I found out why pretty quick.

About a block in front of me, I saw a woman, a pretty black girl, really. She got out of a cab on the corner and started walking toward a building entrance. By the time I got there, she was almost to the door, and I was about thrity feet away.

This dude got out of a parked car and grabbed at her. She let out a holler that would have raised the dead. And you know? Not a single light went on in any of the apartments facing the street. Not one window rolled up. Almost without thinking, I shot a bolt of *psi* energy at the robber. He stopped like a freeze-frame shot in a movie. He stood there like a statue.

Once the girl saw she was safe, I expected her to dash into the doorway of her building. Uh-uh. She all of a sudden relaxed and walked around the guy, looking him over. Just like you'd walk around a statue in a museum. She took her purse from his immobilized fingers and checked the contents. Satisfied it was all there, she began to wham the daylights out of this dude with her purse, knuckles, and feet! I mean she played a tune on this creep. Finally knocked him down to the pavement. When she had him down, she did a little dance on his face with her heavy, platform-soled shoes. I know it was only fair, but after a while it started to sicken me. The guy's face was beginning to look like hamburger.

I couldn't take any more, so I sent her into her house. Then I went over and checked out the dude on the ground. He was bloody but not badly hurt. I looked into his mind and nearly puked. This guy had a mind like . . . Well, have you ever noticed the bottoms of movie seats in the kids' section? The crap, filth, and corruption stuck to them? That was the inside of this dude's head. Brrrr! I also saw that he was no stranger to attacking chicks, either. Then I got my idea.

I programed him to go to the nearest police station, confess everything, and give himself up. He got to his feet and marched off stiffly toward the nearest station house. I made a mental note to smooth out my technique. That jerky walk. I'd never fool an Eddie Rodriguez with technique like that.

Washington Dispatch

The Cat Surrenders!

March 10—The man who has terrorized the city for the past 18 months with 20 rape-robberies has surrendered to a local precinct house in the Southwest section.

Edward Macon, 32, of 3822 P St., SW, walked into the 120th precinct house at 1:30 this morning. "I'm the Cat. I want to give myself up," he allegedly stated.

Prompt investigation of details furnished by the suspect led to his immediate arrest and arraignment this afternoon. Macon is being held without bail.

Martin Grossman

It was bound to happen. Myra tells me that Luis has been coming and going from the Greenglade complex at will for the past week. In a way, it's frightening. In another, it's consoling. He didn't have to come back here if he didn't want to. Evidently, he did want to. At least he seems to be favoring our cause. Myra feels his only motivation is revenge for his brother's death. I agree. He certainly has no great love for I.G.O. and anyone connected with the Organization. That may include me. Not that I think he bears me any real malice. But he's a practical joker. So easy to forget that he's only sixteen. And kids do like to play games.

Today, we were conducting some tests. The object was to control a subject at maximum distance. Due to the security aspects and limitations of "need to know," I agreed to be the test subject. I went into Washington, hailed a cab, and commenced touring the D.C. area. Luis was to locate me and send me a command to return to Greenglade. Which he did quite well.

The embarrassing part was the detour he put in. I found myself at a noon luncheon for the Daughters of the Confederacy over at the Commodore Hotel. I burst into the room and sang them a fast chorus of *Marching Through Georgia.* For an encore, Luis had me throw the ladies a full moon! I don't know how I escaped arrest. Possibly Luis was controlling the entire situation. He grows more powerful every day.

Priority Ten (10)

Mar. 30

To: Secretary of State

From: G.T. Case, Director, I.G.O. HQ, Greenglade MD.

Re: Ianos Iorga and YPI Church

Dear Mr. Secretary:

It's been so long since I've had good news to report, I'm out of practice. The detector devices are all installed. The Greenglade HQ is now secured.

I think I can safely mention the project I've been so secretive about. We needn't feel we are helpless against NIETZSCHE. We have a NIETZSCHE of our own! He's the brother of Field Agent Ortiz, who was killed in the line of duty investigating Iorga (see persfile attached). Though he's not as strong a *psi*-adept as NIETZSCHE, our resident experts feel he can give NIETZSCHE a good fight. If you add the total resources of I.G.O. to that, we have a formidable counterforce.

Unfortunately, as the subject Ortiz was unaware of his capabilities up until three weeks ago, extensive training had to be done. According to Grossman and Sokolow, he is currently about mid-point in his development. By the time Iorga completes his Long Walk and enters New York, we should be ready for him. We already know his itinerary and the ground we'll be fighting on. That's half the battle there. I am, at this point, guardedly confident. Amplifying reports to follow.

Case

George Case

I feel like some kind of doo-doo! I sent a flash off to the Secretary that things are looking up. The last of the detectors had been installed in the White House. The test figures for Luis Ortiz were getting better every day. I spent my first night at my place in Georgetown in over three months.

I'm getting like a mole here in Greenglade. I was actually nervous being in a civilian house, above ground! And I always thought of myself as an outside operative. I wasn't even sure I wanted the West Coast command when Henskey offered it to me. I must be so whacked out that I'm getting to like it.

I ate a good breakfast at home and arrived at Greenglade at 7:30 A.M. At 9:00 A.M. Grossman came bursting into my office. In one sentence, I was ready to take off for the tall timber. He said quite simply, "Luis Ortiz is missing!"

Renaldo Ortiz

I think I understand what Luis meant. And I think I approve of what he wants to do. This, as a man who knows that there are other things in this world besides his own needs and desires. More important things. As a father, my heart feels like a piece of stone in my breast.

I was reading the paper in my study when Luis walked in the door. I was startled and amazed. I had spoken to him on the telephone an hour earlier. I believed he was in Boston at school. But there is no way to fly from Boston, then drive out to the Hamptons in under an hour. I thought perhaps he had played a joke on me; he had been in town when he called. Then he told me of being near Washington D.C. for the past month.

I have telephoned Luis twice a week at his school. Each time, I have reached him. He told me of the relay system that transfers my calls to Maryland automatically when I dial his Boston number. He also told me the truth about Juanillo's death. And Juanillo's real job with the government. I suppose I should be proud. But all I feel is emptiness and fear. Fear that I may lose still another son—my only son.

There is no doubt that this thing, this *demonio,* must be destroyed. But why must it take my son to do it? And these remarkable things that Luis can do. He showed me how he can move objects; even himself. That is how

111

he was able to be on Long Island after phoning me only an hour before.

I thought that the government people had done something to my son. Something to give him these powers. Luis said no. That he has always had the power. The government people have but taught him how to use it. That may be so, but still they want him to use the power for their ends. To my horror, he has agreed to help them.

He told me the purpose of his visit was to allay my fears. He might have to disappear or change his name. I would not then be able to call him on the telephone. He didn't want me to worry. It is strange what a child thinks will worry a parent. Now that I know what Luis is doing, I worry even more. He is so young.

George Case

He just took a little trip to visit his father! I've been turning the complex and the Eastern seaboard upside down. And he's been having a little chitchat with his father. Swell.

Grossman and Sokolow tell me that he's been coming and going from Greenglade whenever he feels like it. Why the hell didn't it show up on the *psi* detectors when he passed them at the exits? Neither of the good doctors have an explanation for that one. It gives me the shudders. If Luis can do it, so can NIETZSCHE. My whole security for HQ and the White House is breaking down. I should report the *psi* detector failure to the

Secretary of State immediately. I have given Grossman and Sokolow twenty-four hours to find out what went wrong with the detectors.

Oddly enough, Ortiz is acting more co-operative than before. He seems to have set his mind on excelling at every test Sokolow and Grossman dream up for him. Today, when I went down to the *psi* lab, which used to be the old ODIN display-console room, Ortiz was running a 40 hp. electric motor, no wires connected to it. While he was doing that, he was also playing a chess game with a small computer. Just for fun, he was reading a physics text between moves! I was impressed and said so.

"Baby stuff," Ortiz said. "Rodriguez is so far ahead of this kind of thing."

"I guess so," I said. "I have seen demonstration films from the Soviet Union, where a *psi*-adept runs a bigger motor than that. But I always assumed it was a doctored film."

"Oh, I'm not just running the thing," Ortiz said jabbing a thumb over his shoulder at the racing motor. "It has a frozen bearing. What I'm doing is providing a friction-free molecular film around the frozen bearing and making the motor put out more than the forty horses it's rated at. At the same time, I'm monitoring all thoughts of passersby in the outside waiting area and playing this machine a not-too-challenging game. I think it's the Fisher-Spassky second game."

He moved a piece on the board. "And that's checkmate!" he said. The computer readout of the chessboard flashed LOSS, then re-cleared. A new game flashed on the read-out screen. He glanced at the screen briefly. He punched out some moves rapidly,

113

then snorted, *"Kieseritzky's Gambit.* This machine is an amateur. Don't we have any interesting games in the program library, Dr. Grossman?"

"You've been playing against nothing but grand masters for the past week, Luis," said Grossman.

"No, I haven't," came back Ortiz. "I've been playing a machine programmed with grand masters' games. A real grand master wouldn't have a chance against me. I could read his strategy and next move before he made it. But it passes the time."

"Speaking of passing the time," I said, "the doctors tell me that you've been taking little pleasure trips away from Greenglade. It has to stop."

The kid grinned at me. "Fine," he smiled. "Who's going to stop me?"

I stood there with egg on my face. The kid was right. There's no one in the world who can stop Luis Ortiz from doing anything he pleases. But I did have an answer.

"NIETZSCHE can stop you," I said. "Your training isn't complete. What would have happened if you had run into Rodriguez in your travels?"

"Then we would have found out how good my training has been, wouldn't we?" replied Ortiz. He made two fast moves on the computer board, then turned in his chair to face me.

"Listen, man," Ortiz said, "I'm helping out you cloak-and-dagger types for one reason. I want the guy that killed my brother. The rest of your concerns are just that: *your* worries, not mine. Frankly, I don't care if this place blows up tomorrow. Long as I'm not in it when it goes." His dark eyes were like those of a wild animal as he said it. "Like Dr. Sokolow," he continued, "I'm

114

not sure that agencies like this should even exist. Secret Police are Secret Police, no matter what you call them."

I turned angrily to Sokolow. "You have no right to impose your opinions on this boy," I snapped. "If you have any counter-productive feelings about this project, I'd appreciate your keeping them to yourself."

Both Sokolow and Ortiz laughed aloud. "And how do you suggest I keep my feelings from a telepath?" she asked smiling.

I know when I'm whipped. I just walked back to my office and dictated three minutes of uninterrupted oaths and obscenities into my steno machine. Then I erased it all and went to lunch.

Cleveland Times

Iorga Performs Mass Nuptials, Then Feeds All Present

March 24—Rumanian holy man Ianos Iorga obliged his followers by performing a mass marriage ceremony today.

Since the beginning of Iorga's Long Walk to New York, a number of young people in his wake have been evidently doing more than just praying and walking. Some of them have fallen in love.

Obligingly, Iorga has married some 50-odd couples who have obtained the necessary papers.

Ceremonies were held at the giant picnic ground at the Ohio State Park near Painesville on Lake Erie.

Once performed, the rites lacked only one thing—a traditional wedding breakfast.

As if by miracle, a truck carrying a trailerload

of bread, cakes, and pies to a nearby market center turned into the park's parking field. The driver opened the trailer doors and invited all present to an impromptu feast.

As it's early in the season, water to the park's over 200 drinking fountains had not been turned on. But for reasons unexplained by park authorities, all of the fountains were in top working order.

The main control valves for the fountains are in a locked building some distance away from the wedding site. A Parks Department spokesman insists that the locks were not tampered with, nor was there any sign of forcible entry to the building. The spokesman also insists that when he checked the site, the valves were still turned off and locked.

Rafael Guzman

He's gonna be here by Easter! He called me on the phone last night. Funny, at first I didn't recognize his voice. But then he told me he got the flu. I know what that's like. Pablo, his wife, and the kids all have it. I don't feel so swell, either. But I did like Eddie said to. The furniture was delivered to the Sheepshead Bay place today. I had to lose a day from the store to be there. So naturally, they come at five o'clock. I could of put in most of a working day and still been there.

It's good stuff, what Eddie ordered. Came from Bloomingdale's. I hope Eddie is gonna move to New York again. Even if he's out here in Brooklyn, I can at least see him once in a while.

I mean, I never got a real chance to thank him for all he done for me and Pablo. And Eddie can get to meet my Luisa. If the store keeps going the way it is, me and Luisa are gonna get married this year. I want Eddie to be best man. Because to me, that's what he always was, the best man. I hope he likes weddings. I don't remember either one of us ever going to one.

Philadelphia Times

Did Iorga Raise the Dead?

CAMDEN, April 1—Continuing his policy of not entering major cities on his world-famed Long Walk, Ianos Iorga held a mass rally across the river in Philadelphia's sister city.

Crowd containment was nearly impossible, due to the number of the faithful who arrived by train and air from cities as distant as Boston and Richmond, Va.

It was because of the overcrowding that Mrs. Elsie Kramm, of Bayonne, N.J., collapsed. Mrs. Kramm, a 42-year-old housewife, has a long history of heart disease, authorities disclosed. At the height of the crush, she fell to the ground, some hundred yards from the platform where Iorga was speaking. Standby medical equipment provided by the city of Camden was on the spot and C.P.R. techniques were immediately employed. Ten minutes later, Mrs. Kramm was pronounced dead by Dr. Charles Bacon of Philadelphia, who was attending the Iorga rally.

Noting the disturbance during his sermon, Iorga went to the scene immediately after his talk ended. Attendants were in the process of removing Mrs. Kramm's body to the Camden Morgue.

Iorga approached Mrs. Kramm's body and removed the covering. Spectators say he then placed his hands on Mrs. Kramm's body, gazed skyward, and fell silent.

As the silence grew unbearable, Iorga finally

117

spoke. "Rise and walk!" he commanded. And Mrs. Kramm did just that!

Medical authorities in the Philadelphia area have declined comment. One doctor, who wishes to remain anonymous, pointed out that mistakes do occur in diagnosing death in coronary cases. "Revivals are not uncommon," he said.

But you can't prove it by Mrs. Elsie Kramm. She is quoted as saying shortly after her resuscitation, "Brother Ianos is not a saint. He is the new Messiah, come to redeem us all."

Iorga, meanwhile, is continuing his Long Walk and is expected to enter New York City on Palm Sunday.

Luis Ortiz

I'm scared. Scared green. I couldn't resist the opportunity to see Iorga, or Rodriguez. Whatever you want to call him. I took a car and drove up to Camden. I could have just as easy walked for all the traffic leading into town. Finally had to leave the car. Let Case's boys return to get it. I'm not going back there until I'm sure Iorga's nowhere near.

I caught his show when he "healed" that woman. I know how he did it too. Right up there from the platform, he scanned the crowd. To have the right dramatic effect, he needed somebody close to him. When he found the Kramm woman in the crowd, he reached out with a *psi* bolt and slowed her heart to a point where that doctor couldn't pick it up on his stethoscope. Rodriguez/Iorga knew there wouldn't be an EKG machine in that ambulance. Then when he was good and ready, he went over and "raised her from the

118

dead." It was a parlor trick, plain and simple. I could have done it myself. But it's the coldness of this dude that gets me. He could just as easily have killed that lady with that cheap stunt. But that's not what scared me. He knew I was there! And he didn't care one little bit.

I was watching his stunt with that lady, figuring out how he did it. I was just giving him a few points for a flashy trick, when he spoke to me mentally. "YES, LUIS, IT'S A TRICK" came the voice inside my head. "BUT THIS IS NO TRICK."

I felt a grip like a clammy vise close over my chest. I couldn't get a breath. I stood rooted and sweating. As the black dots started floating in front of my eyes, I knew I was going to die. Right then and there.

"COMFORTABLE, LUIS?" came the voice. "WHAT IF I SQUEEZE YOU A BIT MORE, NOW?"

The pain in my chest became unbearable. It felt like my heart was going to burst inside my rib cage. I don't know whether it was the *psi* bolt I tried to get off that stopped it, or if he was tired of the game. He let go of me. I fell to the ground like I didn't have a bone in my body. Some people nearby tried to help me. Iorga's kids, most of them. As I got to my feet, I heard his voice again.

"TELL GEORGE CASE NOT TO SEND CHILDREN TO STOP ME. I HAVE DECIDED TO ALLOW YOU TO LIVE, SO YOU MAY DELIVER MY MESSAGE. IF I FIND YOU IN MY WAY AGAIN, I'LL CRUSH YOU LIKE A BUG!"

I panicked. Soon as I was loose of that *thing's* grip, I teleported back to Greenglade. In a cold sweat. Now, I have to tell Sokolow and Grossman. I don't think I can handle this guy!

Martin Grossman

"Rubbish, utter rubbish!" Myra said to Luis Ortiz. The boy was seated on his bed, his head cradled in his hands. He had called us in a few minutes after returning to Greenglade from Camden. He told us the whole story. He was ready to quit. Not a question of physical courage, either. The boy is brave. He went to Camden to check out the enemy. I wouldn't have.

"Don't you see?" Myra continued. "If he were able to kill you, Eddie would have done it on the spot. He is merciless. When he lashed out at you, it was with the complete intention of killing. He needs no messengers to threaten George Case. When he realized that he couldn't destroy you, he tried to psych you into believing he could. Although you did a foolish thing, going near him before you were prepared properly, I am actually encouraged by this turn of events. At least I know you are not in mortal danger."

"But he had other things on his mind at the same time," Luis protested. "He was controlling the crowd and that woman's heartbeat at the same time. I got the feeling that if he had concentrated on just me, he could have wiped me out!"

"And I do not think so," said Myra with finality. "Let us continue with your training program. It's our best hope. With practice, you may be able to combat his power to immobilize you. Today, we concentrate on your control of your own body functions under distracting conditions."

Just then, the door to the room banged open. A marine guard stepped into the room and leveled a .45 automatic at Luis' head! Luis glanced at the marine casually. The armed man's gun flew across the room and clattered to the floor. At the same time, he slipped to the floor, unconscious. Luis got to his feet and looked down at the inert form. He crouched down and took the man's face between his hands.

"He's dead," said Ortiz in a low voice. "But I didn't kill him," he continued. "I only disarmed him."

"Then how?" I began.

"He was being controlled from a distance," said Ortiz. "Quiet! I'm trying to pick up his last thoughts. His brain isn't dead yet. It's dying though."

We sat in silence as Luis stayed where he was, still holding the dead guard. Finally, he released the body and gently lowered its head to the floor. He looked up and sighed deeply. Then he said, "I have to leave this place. It's too dangerous here. Rodriguez reached out and took over this poor guy. It happened in microseconds. I almost didn't have time to react. When Rodriguez felt me disarm the guard, he burst some blood vessels in the poor dude's brain. That's what killed him."

"But why leave?" I asked. "He didn't get you."

"Don't you see?" said Ortiz impatiently. "He's trying to get me, like Myra said. But he's taking no more chances on me fighting back. It was a long shot trying to get me the way he did. I handled it. But what if it had been a whole squad of marines with automatic weapons? No, there are too many armed men in this complex for me to take any more chances."

"But surely, you aren't going to let him run you off this way?" I said.

"You misunderstand, Martin," said Myra quietly. "Luis doesn't want any more innocent people killed. He himself was not in any great danger. We were."

I looked at Ortiz, and he nodded his agreement. "I have to leave, you see," he said. "And I can't tell you where I'm going. I haven't decided yet. If I had, Myra would know from my thoughts. I'll give you an address to send the rest of my training program to. I know the post office box co-ordinates; I'll pick them up by *psi.* It's for your own protection."

And with that, just like you turn off a light switch, Luis Ortiz disappeared into thin air. The only trace of his going was a popping sound, as the air in the room rushed into the vacuum formed by his departure.

Myra and I looked at each other for a while. Then she smiled and said, "Now we must go to see George Case and tell him that his secret weapon has . . . how do you say it? Taken a powder?"

Priority Ten (10)

Apr. 4

To: All Operatives, ALL OFFICES

From: G.T. Case, Director, I.G.O. HQ, Greenglade, MD.

Re: Luis Ortiz

COMPLETE ID DOSSIER ACCOMPANIES THIS ORDER. FIND THIS MAN IMMEDIATELY. THIS IS A PRIORITY TEN MATTER. IF THIS MAN, ORTIZ, IS SPOTTED, *DO NOT ATTEMPT TO DETAIN HIM! MAKE NO ATTEMPT AT COMMUNICATION!* SIMPLY REPORT WHEREABOUTS OF THIS SUBJECT TO ANY LOCAL I.G.O. INSTALLATION IMMEDIATELY. LOCATION OF THIS SUBJECT URGENT TO INTERNATIONAL SECURITY. FIRST OPERATIVE TO REPORT SUBJECT'S LOCATION WILL BE UPGRADED TWO FULL POINTS IN RANK, PAY, AND PRIVILEGE.

George Case

I'm whistling in the dark, and I know it. If Ortiz wants to do a Houdini, I can't think of a way to find him. Any more than I could locate NIETZSCHE if he didn't want to be found. Face it, the kid can make himself appear to be anyone or anything. Even if one of my agents stumbles across him, if Ortiz notices, he can erase the agent's memories of the sighting. I know. NIETZSCHE did it to us a couple of times before Henskey realized what he was up against.

But I have to do something! Saw the paper today. Tomorrow is Palm Sunday, and NIETZSCHE will be in New York. The YPI has rented Yankee Stadium for Easter Sunday and two days after. They can't seat all the kids at one session. I have a week to locate Ortiz and make a war plan. A week! I need years.

123

Martin Grossman

Luis may or may not be in New York City. Today, we received the post office box number. It's at Grand Central. Smart move. It's open twenty-four hours. Eddie may have the box watched, if he knows about it. But he can't watch it himself, twenty-four hours a day. And anyone else, Luis can fake out with a different appearance. I wanted to send the rest of the materials to him by special courier. Case says no. It would draw attention to that particular box. Which is the last thing we need. It will have to go by mail. At least it can be Special Delivery. I wonder where Luis is?

The Dalai Lama

What a charming boy. And so respectful as befits his years. He did startle my poor priests arriving that way. At first I didn't notice him. I was deep in prayer and meditation when he arrived. But as I was gradually emerging from my state, I became aware of the disturbance in my chamber. They are good men, my priests, but ignorant. As he arrived by using mental force, they assumed him to be some saint or holy person. However, once I perceived his powers, I was able to say to them, "Fear not, my children. This is but a man. Leave us." It made them feel better.

The boy told me of his struggle with the powers of

darkness. I, of course, am not interested in temporal things. I advised him to stay here with me and to concentrate on the true nature of the universe.

He is being consumed by this idea of revenge for his brother's death. An unworthy motive. It will not return his brother to him. But he is young and unlearned. Some day, perhaps, he will return, and we will share the mysteries of creation together. I know I have met my soul's brother.

He asked a simple thing of me. I was happy to oblige him. He only wished to merge consciousness with me. "May I enter your being?" he asked. If only he knew the loneliness I daily endure, he needn't have asked. I welcomed communion with him. I first took him to the end of the universe, where the consciousness of Buddha starts and ends. We watched a star die, the light filling the void for a time, then the roaring wrath of God as it exploded. Next, we drifted through the currents of time and space, reflecting on its wonders. After a time we returned. He has learned what he wanted to learn. He asked no more of me. I bless this boy and await his return. He will guide my successor when I move to another plane of existence.

New York Tribune

Brother Ianos Enters the City, Thousands Line His Path.

April 7—Today, the Long Walk of Ianos Iorga, begun in November of last year as a pilgrimage to revive religion in the United States, is almost ended. The Rumanian holy man has trekked 3000 miles to culminate the walk at Yankee Stadium on Easter Sunday.

As Iorga strolled across the George Washington Bridge, the city of New York did its best. Thousands of the faithful were stationed at various points along his route down upper Broadway and finally midtown to the former Viking Hotel, now YPI's Eastern headquarters.

As to how many people will attend the three-day prayer meeting which begins on Easter Sunday, a spokesman for the New York Hotel Operators' Association commented, "There's not a bed in New York for the next week."

Excerpt from Multi-media News, (Channel 6), WBC-TV

ANCHOR MAN: And here now to give you his impressions of Brother Ianos Iorga's New York visit is Al Grossman.

AL: Thank you, Will, and good evening. Well, Brother Ianos has finally arrived in New York City, and this reporter, for one, is unimpressed. As is his habit, Iorga managed to have crowds of his followers interfere with TV cameramen, and declined direct interviews with all but the newspapers. *(Roll film of procession.)* This consistently veiled hostility toward the electronic news media accounts for some of the sketchy quality of our film. At this point, you will see that our cameraman was "accidentally" knocked to the ground by the adoring crowds trying to catch a glimpse of what some are hailing as "The New Messiah."

I attempted to get closer and speak a few words as

126

Iorga entered the main entrance of the YPI Church headquarters at the former Viking Hotel on West 79th Street. But Iorga was ringed by the ever-present goon squad of clean, smiling young people. They politely and smilingly refused to allow any TV news person near Iorga. *(End film.)* It's not for me to disparage any religious movement. But I question seriously the methods of Ianos Iorga. Last month, after still another Yippie death in Kansas City, I called for a serious investigation of the YPI Church. To date, our letters and calls to the Federal Bureau of Investigation have received the same reply: "This department has conducted an investigation of the organization to which you refer. We find nothing to indicate any cause for alarm or further investigation."

What does the FBI consider cause for alarm? How about the three deaths, no, four deaths, in the wake of Iorga's Long Walk? Who has looked into the connection between phantom oilman and financier Edward Saunders and the YPI Church? What is the source of income for the YPI Church besides the kids on corners who sell you candy for so-called contributions? All these questions and more remain unanswered. There will be a media blackout of the services scheduled at Yankee Stadium on Easter Sunday. But I for one will be there, along with staff artist Joe Buongiorno, who will bring you his sketches of the holy clambake in the Bronx. This is Al Grossman. Now, back to Will McCrae.

127

Luis Ortiz

I love that old Chinese man. I don't know what made me think of it, going there to see him. It must have been that article I read on him a few years back. It didn't make sense to me then. It sure does now.

For years, in Tibet, each time a Dalai Lama dies, his priests go into neighboring villages to find the boy whose body the Lama's spirit has entered. That boy then becomes the new Dalai Lama. I wrote it off as superstition and reincarnation. I didn't recognize the pattern, that's all.

For hundreds of years now, a visitor from the future has lived in Tibet! He has occupied and shared the bodies and minds of young Tibetan boys for generations. And each year, he's grown more knowledgeable and, if possible, more powerful. If I needed advice, why not get it from a being who has centuries of experience?

It also proved to me that this business of sharing my life with something alien doesn't have to end up a horror story. And so far as I know, I've never had any contact with my visitor. It's been with me since I was born. I feel no different than before I knew about it. I feel exactly like Luis Jesús Ortiz. The Lama says that the creature that entered Ianos Iorga, and Eddie Rodriguez before that, is probably insane. Myra Sokolow says that monsters like Hitler, Caligula, Attila—all those fun guys—were occupied by insane visitors.

I felt that this business of dumping a future society's misfits and rejects on us back here was a bummer. And if these future dudes are so intelligent and responsible, how can they permit the terrible things their rejects do to the world?

The Lama says it doesn't matter. It's already part of history up then in the future. What has been will be. That kind of thing. I asked him if Rodriguez can be destroyed. He wasn't interested. But he did say that what will happen has already happened. Which was swell, but didn't tell me much.

I told him I was going back to fight Rodriguez. He wished me well. I'm still scared, but the Lama said something to me before I split. He said, "We shall meet again." Swell for him to say. I don't know if he meant he'd meet me or my visitor in another life.

George Case

It's three days to Easter Sunday. Where is Ortiz? I have this sinking feeling that Iorga/NIETZSCHE got him. I keep checking the news clipping department. I've personally read any account in the past few weeks of unidentified bodies being found. Bodies that fit the general description of Luis Ortiz. Two leads, both wrong. I can only assume that we've lost him. I don't know how I'll face Ortiz' father. Two sons dead (that is, if he, Luis, is dead) and both under my orders at the time. I feel like I did back when I was a second lieutenant in Korea. All those letters back home that I wrote.

But if I'm going to lose to NIETZSCHE, I'm going down swinging. I've been in touch with Monsignor Gaxton at

Loyola in Chicago. The exorcist should be arriving in New York tonight at 7:00 P.M. It took hours on the phone with Gaxton, but I finally convinced him. The pattern Iorga has followed leaves little doubt. It's an old term, but I feel it applies to Iorga/NIETZSCHE: The Antichrist!

Martin Grossman

For once, Case has come up with a workable idea. Even Myra approves, but for a completely different set of reasons. When Case first broached the subject of exorcism, I nearly laughed. Not Myra. She told Case she thought it was an excellent idea. After Case left to make arrangements, I said to Myra, "Do you really believe that an exorcist can do anything? Or did you just want Case out of our hair?"

"Two questions, Martin. First, do I believe in all the dogma and trappings that surround exorcism? No, I do not. Second, do I believe that an exorcist could be of help in combatting Eddie Rodriguez? That answer is yes."

"But Christian . . . Gentile rites. You don't believe in that."

"Ah, but I do, Martin. Not in the religion, but in the effects of exorcism. As we both know, demonic possession is an improper merging of a future visitor and a human of today. Or years ago. My point is that so-called demons *have* been cast out of host bodies and minds over the years. As to the sectarian aspect, there is an

130

equivalent ceremony of exorcism in our faith, Islam, and Christianity. Primitive religions abound in such rites."

"But we know that the nature of Iorga's possession isn't demonic. It's well, what it is. How can exorcism help?" I asked.

"I believe that the key to its usefulness depends on the strength of belief of the exorcist. Look at the way Eddie disposed of the priest Case had called in months ago. He destroyed the airplane, and in the process, the priest. He simply could have taken over the priest's mind and sent the man back to New York. He didn't do that. Why?"

"So he could get Johnny Ortiz at the same time?" I offered.

"I don't think so," Myra said. "I think that if a potential victim of a creature like Eddie has an unshakeable religious conviction, he cannot be moved by any force, *psi* or temporal."

"But I've read histories of possession where the victim was a priest. Urban Grandier was burned at the stake in Loudon, France, in the seventeenth century, and he was a priest."

"I'm familiar with the case you cite, Martin," said Myra. "I seem to recall that Grandier was hardly a faithful servant of God. In fact, among other accusations, he was supposed to have had relations with a number of nuns in the Loudon convent. I think he was possessed because he didn't have the faith to resist."

"Then, what is it you're proposing, Myra?"

"I think that we should put together a team of exorcists of many different faiths. And with me acting as their guide to Eddie Rodriguez and funneling all their faith (which is a form of *psi* energy, I believe) at Iorga/Eddie, we may be able to fight him."

"And win?" I asked.

"I didn't say we could win. I said we could at least try to fight him."

I didn't mention aloud my personal fear of Eddie. Myra has been working on my claustrophobia for two years. I think I could even take being caught between floors in an elevator now. But Eddie knows my weakness. He once capitalized on it and would do so again.

Myra misses nothing. "I know you're frightened, Martin," she said. "And despite your fears, you are still going along with me to face Eddie. I have seen bravery of all sorts in my lifetime, but yours is the noblest. You place yourself in jeopardy for the love of another."

"Myra," I began, "it doesn't seem the time to say it, but . . ."

"Yes, I know," she replied smiling at me. "We have no secrets, you and I." She took my hand.

"Well, do you mind, then, if a non-telepath says his feelings aloud?" I said.

"Not at all."

"I love you, Myra. As I've loved no other person in my life."

"And I love you, Martin."

I felt like a kid who gets the most beautiful birthday cake in the world. Hearing Myra speak what we both felt, yet had never articulated, was everything I wanted to know or hear. Then I thought of the trip to New York and what awaited us. The kid had just got his face pushed into the beautiful cake.

Selim Bakka

I trust this strange little middle-aged woman. When she came to me and said she had the true circumstances of Jasmin's death, I thought she might have been one of the media jackals. When she told me that she could read my thoughts, I almost threw her and Dr. Grossman out. I thank several gods that although the years have taught me prudence, they have not crippled me with caution.

This remarkable white woman can do all she says. Furthermore, I believe what she says about Ianos Iorga. It all fits. This story she tells of visitors from the future, beings of pure mental energy, that is another matter. Possession by devils, I understand. It is part of my childhood religion. After all, was not my father a chief and my uncle a shaman? I have assisted at the casting out of demons before. I know as well as any shaman the chants and what I need—the powders, the herbs. I will go with this woman and face whatever devil killed my Jasmin. And if I lose my soul in the process, so be it.

For what is left to me? I have no son. I have land, cattle. I have respect from my brothers in Islam, though I am a poor Moslem. It is all ashes in my mouth. I have a responsibility to my people. To represent them at the U.N. But I am not deceived. I was named to this post to keep me out of the internal affairs of Dakama. My constant taking of causes in the name of the back country population made me too powerful not to hold office. Too well known to assassinate and too meddlesome to keep in Dakama. So, *voilà!* I become a U.N. ambassador. I have done much for my people. I have had a full life. Now, I will face this devil and see the color of his white skin.

Martin Grossman

How in the world would Myra know how to get hold of a Chasidic rabbi? She's about as religious as I am. I expected a hassle from Shlomo Jacobs. Nothing of the sort. When Myra told him she had a case of a *dibbuk* inhabiting a victim, he only nodded and asked for more particulars! I suppose that the world is still full of wonders to the *Chasidim.*

Pietro Carbone

The Monsignor says this appears to be a case of genuine possession and requires an experienced exorcist. There's no doubt I am that. But I've never met Satan or a demon. Every case I've been called in on has had another logical scientific explanation. And there seem to be more cases each year. If only the ignorant would pay more attention to their own lives and actions and less to crying "Devil!" when something seems inexplicable.

I believe this preoccupation on the part of the laity with demons and devils is unhealthy. It's probably just a fad, this delving into the occult. But I believe I see a trend. Over the past ten years, there have been an ever greater number of books and films on the subject. Impressionable minds have picked it up and made the occult a sort of subculture. But I must go and investigate; it's my duty. For what if, this one time, we really *are* dealing with Satan?

Memo

To: All Personnel Assigned

From: G.T. Case, Director, I.G.O. HQ, Greenglade, MD.

Re: Ianos Iorga/YPI Rally at Yankee Stadium

All agents will remain at their assigned duty posts unless specifically ordered elsewhere by me IN PERSON. No telephone or radio changes will be made nor radio frequencies changed. Once you are in place, no runners or messengers will be sent. Disregard any such.

Under no circumstances will you take any action not contained in plans Beta and Alpha. The red signal flare will indicate plan Alpha, the green signal flare, plan Beta.

We anticipate a disturbance of riot magnitude. DO NOT ATTEMPT TO ASSIST WITH CROWD CONTROL. That's the job of the New York City Police. You will remain at your posts until specifically dismissed by me.

Case

135

George Case

And if NIETZSCHE kills me, someone else will relieve them. I have to plan as though I'm going to survive this battle. Otherwise, there's no point in going into it. I've been to see demolition again. The device is in place. This can't be a bluff. It has to be a real one. It's a tactical, low-yield thermonuclear device about the size of a suitcase. The timing is automatic once the flare goes.

But if I have to use it, I will. I know it should take out anywhere from three to four square blocks. And I know NIETZSCHE can't get to the operation site. We have detectors in place that will trigger it if he tries any *psi* monkey business.

Martin Grossman

I should tell Case that those detectors are useless gadgets. The original idea was that Myra would be the real *psi* energy detector. It was fine at the time, but now I think he's placing too much confidence in those gizmos. If he thinks he has a real weapon against Rodriguez, he may do something rash. Something that may cost more lives.

Myra disagrees. She says that as long as Case is distracted with gadgets, he won't be bothering us.

We're due to have a council of war with Selim Bakka and Shlomo Jacobs tonight. That priest Case flew in from Chicago will be sitting in too. I'm surprised. The Catholic Church may talk ecumenism, but this area is very sensitive. When it comes to demons, you can find as many opinions as there are clergymen.

Selim Bakka

I don't trust this situation. I believe we were expected all along. From the beginning, I felt it had a limited chance, but one that had to be taken. Now, I feel we are being led down a chute. Of the sort cattle are run through on the way to the knack hammer.

We had made an early start for Yankee Stadium, knowing that the crowds would be heavy. There was no thought of a police-escorted car or motorcade. In our enthusiasm, we thought there might have been an element of surprise. I had seen the inside of a New York subway train but once. It was with the then-mayor of New York as part of a city tour. I had never been in one of those trains when there were a great number of people. I think I know now what makes New Yorkers the abrupt, surly individuals they are. If I had to ride a crowded subway to and from my work every day, I would be surly too!

We reached the area and hadn't been there long

enough to enter the gates when we were approached by one of the YPI's. She was young, so engaging and kind. She had that same look of serenity and joy that I saw in my poor Jasmin. All around us was a milling sea of young people, all wearing that same, unworldly smile. In a crowd this size in a city like Cairo or Tokyo, we could have expected jostling elbows, and people treading on one's feet. Not here. The young woman who approached us called Dr. Sokolow by name. We halted as a group when she said, "I am Sister Evelyn. Brother Ianos would like to see all of you before he speaks to the multitudes. He is in a dressing room in the basement. Follow me, please."

I heard Case say to Dr. Grossman, "Don't worry. I still hold a high card or two."

Dr. Sokolow, whom I know to be telepathic, looked as though she had been struck in the face. She obviously read something in Case's mind. Something terrible. But what?

George Case

Sokolow thinks I'm insane. Well, maybe I am. I've fought with NIETZSCHE before. I remember how he used a thermonuclear device as blackmail. Two can do that. It was unproductive of Sokolow to say what she did. It was almost as though she could read my mind. I was thinking of the device I had planted. She looked at me and said, "Mr. Case, you are mad! Conventional weapons are useless against this creature. All you have

138

done is endanger a hundred thousand lives. And by the way, those detectors you trust so much are useless."

I had no time for a reply. We were already deep below Yankee Stadium and approaching the dressing room door. Behind it was NIETZSCHE. Sokolow was busy conferring with the three exorcists. As the door swung open, all I could think of was that phrase I used to hear some comic say on TV: "NOW she tells me . . ."

Martin Grossman

As the door swung open, it all came rushing back. The way Eddie had played upon my claustrophobia before. We were deep below the stadium. I was already nervous from walking through the ill-lighted rabbit runs that form a labyrinth below the section of the stadium the public never sees. I thought of darkened rooms. I thought of the time I had been trapped for two days in that cave-in so many years ago, when I thought spelunking was a great hobby. I felt ready to bolt. Then Myra put her hand in mine and I felt better.

I'd never seen Ianos Iorga in person. I realized instantly why Iorga had ruled out most TV news people. It wasn't just that the *psi* effects don't carry to a TV camera to influence them. It had to do with Iorga's physical size. In Rumania, I suppose, Iorga would be of average height. But here in the States, where diet is better, our people are, on the average, much taller. Iorga is well under six feet tall. That doesn't inspire a godlike image in the United States. I think this is the only country in the world where men consider being over six feet tall a personal accomplishment. But if he was discomfited being the shortest person in the room except for Myra, Iorga didn't show it. He smiled broadly as we entered and said, "Myra, how good to see you again. Oh! And Dr. Grossman, your faithful dog. Still sniffing after Myra, eh, Grossman? And let's not forget old Stinky Case! You don't know how I've looked forward to this, Case."

I don't know what Iorga/Rodriguez would have said next. Myra gave him no chance. I heard her mental command to Father Carbone. He stepped forward holding a crucifix before him and intoned, "I exorcise thee, most vile spirit, in the name of Jesus Christ, to flee from this creature of God. I bring you the words of Him who commands the sea, the winds, the tempests. Hear, therefore, and fear, Oh Satan, enemy of the faith, foe to the human race, thief of life, root of evil. I adjure thee, vile serpent, to depart instantly. Remember, it is God who commands thee, Christ who commands thee; the Holy Ghost commands thee. Go out, thou transgressor, *draco nequissime,* depart from this man NOW!"

"Now, Selim!" cried Myra, and Selim Bakka threw off his topcoat and tore off the *dashiki* he wore beneath it. In that instant, Bakka was a man transformed. He wore a simple loincloth, and his body was painted in stripes of red, white, and black pigments. Despite the chill of the underground dressing room, his body glistened. Perhaps it was oil; I couldn't say. A pouch of leather was at his waist and from his coat he produced a wand that was part club, part rattle. It had an uncommonly ugly demon head carved into the root knot that formed its end. He began to chant, and as he did, he threw the powdery contents of the pouch at his waist squarely into Iorga/Rodriguez' face. Iorga reeled, as though physically struck.

"Now, Reb!" cried Myra, and Shlomo Jacobs cast off his coat and stepped forward. The short, round man was dressed in the manner of the ancient Russian rabbinate: white from head to foot. A long, silk *tallith* fell to his feet. His head was covered with the traditional fur-trimmed *streimal.* In one hand, he held a sturdy palm frond, a *lulav.* In his other hand was a *shofar,* the ram's horn. He began to speak in Hebrew, in a voice so rich and deep that it seemed to come from the soles of his feet.

"In the name of the forty-two letters of the God with long sight, I adjure thee, abject spirit, *dibbuk* from Hell, to get thee out from residence in the body of this man! Wilt thou, or wilt thou not reply?"

It may have been imagination on my part, but the lights in the dressing room seemed to dim. The atmosphere, so cold earlier, became almost tropical, and the scent of Bakka's oils and powders was strong in the air. But it was working! Iorga put a hand before his eyes, as if to shield them from a bright light. He began backing toward a dressing table behind him. The three exorcists moved relentlessly toward Iorga, each intoning his own rite. Rabbi Jacobs was stalking Iorga as a mongoose does a cobra.

"What is thy name?" thundered Jacobs to the *dibbuk* he knew resided within Iorga. "Make thyself known and begone!"

Without warning, Shlomo Jacobs put the *shofar* to his lips and blew a blast that seemed to rock the foundations of the great stadium. He began to strike Iorga with the *lulav* he carried. Iorga sank to the floor.

George Case stepped forward and cried, "That's it. Give it to the bastard. Let him have it! More! More!" shouted Case. "Make him crawl!"

I saw Iorga/Rodriguez on the floor, face down. I couldn't believe our luck. Or maybe it wasn't luck. Maybe that many men of God in one room somehow did reach the ear of the Deity. No matter what name each of them called Him. The shoulders of Iorga/Rodriguez' inert body began to quiver, then shake. Myra called for the exorcists to cease chanting. The little dressing room fell silent. All eyes were on the quaking form lying on the floor.

"We got him!" crowed Case. "He's crying! He's actually weeping!"

"I think not," said Myra in a flat voice. "Look."

Iorga/Rodriguez, still shaking, had rolled over and was now face up. There were tears in his eyes, all right. From laughter. He was rolling around the floor now. Great hysterical peals of laughter rolled from his lips. The mocking laughter was more than an aural phenomenon now. It echoed telepathically inside my head. It grew louder, louder, intolerably louder. The world, the room, the inside of our heads echoed to that obscene, sarcastic laugh. I saw the Catholic priest reach to his breast and clutch at his crucifix. He held it before him and walked up to where Iorga/Rodriguez lay on the floor laughing.

"Noli me tangere, Satanas," he intoned. It only set Rodriguez off into fresh gales of laughter. With some difficulty and still shaking, he put his hand on the dressing table and got to his feet. Wiping the tears of laugh-

142

ter from his eyes, he turned and addressed us all telepathically. The voice thundered in our minds.

"ENOUGH! DON'T MAKE ME LAUGH ANY MORE. I HAVE TO ADDRESS ALL THOSE SIMPLETONS OUT THERE IN A FEW MINUTES. IF I THINK OF YOU DUNG-EATING INSECTS BACK HERE, I'M LIABLE TO FALL DOWN LAUGHING AGAIN. AND HOW WOULD THAT LOOK? THE NEW MESSIAH ROLLING AROUND ON A STAGE IN THE MIDDLE OF YANKEE STADIUM. OH, HO-HO, HA-HA-HA-HA!"

And he was off again, with that maniacal laugh. As abruptly as if a switch were thrown, he stopped and his face darkened. He gazed at us all like a butterfly collector looks at specimens.

"I'VE ALLOWED YOU PIECES OF DIRT TO COME HERE AND SHARE MY GLORIOUS PRESENCE. I ESPECIALLY WANT GEORGE CASE TO ENJOY THIS MOMENT WITH ME. GOOD OLD STINKY. YOU MORON! I FIND YOU AND YOUR SILLY LITTLE AGENCY LAUGHABLE. DID YOU THINK I WASN'T MILES AHEAD OF YOU EVERY STEP OF THE WAY? DO YOU THINK FOR AN INSTANT THAT YOUR PRECIOUS PSI DETECTORS WERE ANYTHING BUT EXPENSIVE JUNK?"

"I'll have my day, Rodriguez," gritted Case.

"YOU HAD YOUR DAY TWO WEEKS AGO, CASE," mocked Rodriguez. "THAT WAS THE FIRST OF THIS MONTH: APRIL FOOL'S DAY!" And again he laughed. "DO YOU THINK I DON'T KNOW THAT YOU HAVE A LOW-YIELD NUKE PLANTED IN THE SUBWAY STATION? DO YOU THINK I HAVEN'T ALREADY NEUTRALIZED YOUR PERSONNEL? IN A FEW MINUTES, WHEN I CALL FOR THE FAITHFUL TO AP-

PROACH ME UP IN THE STADIUM, THE FORTY AGENTS YOU HAVE OUT THERE WILL BE AMONG THE FIRST!"

Case looked as though someone had first shot his dog, then his mother. Rodriguez/Iorga's announcement, whether true or not, had completely demoralized him. He leaned back against the dressing room wall as though he had been dealt a physical blow.

"I SEE YOU'RE THINKING THAT THERE WILL BE A LAST-MINUTE RESCUE, CASE. DON'T BOTHER YOURSELF. YOUR AGENCY HAS BEEN NEUTRAL-IZED. THE NEW FBI CHIEF HAS BEEN UNDER MY INFLUENCE SINCE TWO MONTHS BEFORE HE WAS NAMED. THAT'S WHY YOU'VE HEARD NO MORE FROM THE FBI ABOUT ME. THERE ISN'T A MAN, WOMAN, OR CHILD IN ANY AGENCY YOU CAN NAME THAT I CAN'T REACH. BUT I DON'T HAVE TO! THAT'S THE BEST, MOST DELICIOUS PART. YOU SEE, STINKY, NOBODY WANTS TO HARM OR HURT ME. EVERYONE LOVES ME."

I heard Myra's reply inside my mind. "They could have loved you, Eddie. That's the sad part. You had it within your grasp to do good with your powers. You could have resolved the conflicts of the world with peace and love. We often talked of it, remember?"

"AH, A WORD FROM JUDAS!" said Rodriguez, turning to face Myra. "NO, I HAVEN'T FORGOTTEN. AND I HAVEN'T FORGOTTEN HOW YOU BETRAYED ME A FEW YEARS BACK, EITHER. BY NOW, THE WORLD WOULD HAVE BEEN AT PEACE. I COULD HAVE OBLITERATED WAR, DISEASE, AND FAMINE. YOU WOULD HAVE HAD A SET OF UNIFORM LAWS, NO NATIONAL BORDERS, FREE TRADE. YOU

144

WOULD HAVE HAD TRUE CONTACT WITH YOUR RULER."

"I would have died first!" cried George Case.

Iorga laughed again. "OH CASE," his voice mocked. "WHY DO YOU PERSECUTE ME AND MINE?"

Case let out an animal cry and pressed his hands to his face. "I'm blind!" he shrieked. "I can't see!" Case began flailing about with his arms. He might have hurt himself or some of the rest of us in the room, but Rodriguez/Iorga sped a *psi* bolt at him that froze him to the spot.

"NOW, NOW, STINKY. WE CAN'T HAVE YOU DAMAGED. YOU KNOW, AFTER YOU HELPED TO DELAY MY PLANS, I THOUGHT THAT THE NEXT TIME WE MET, I MIGHT NOT KILL YOU. I WAS EVEN TEMPTED TO LET DARRYL HENSKEY LIVE. LET HIM BE TRAPPED INSIDE HIS ROTTING BODY FOR YEARS. I WAS THE ONE THAT CAUSED HIS STROKE. IT'S A SIMPLE MATTER. YOU BURST ENOUGH BLOOD VESSELS IN THE BRAIN, AND YOU CAN TURN AN ACTIVE MAN INTO A VEGETABLE. IT AMUSED ME TO SEE HENSKEY STRUGGLE TO RECOVER THE USE OF HIS RIGHT HAND. EACH TIME HE MADE A LITTLE PROGRESS, I'D PAY HIM ANOTHER VISIT AND CRIPPLE HIM AGAIN. WHEN HE FOUND OUT IT WAS I WHO WAS DOING IT, IT WAS EVEN SWEETER."

"You *are* a monster," breathed Selim Bakka. First words he had said.

"AND YOU ARE BENEATH MY NOTICE," said Iorga. "ANY MORE SPEAKING TO ME, UNLESS YOU ARE DIRECTLY ADDRESSED, AND I WILL STRIKE YOU DUMB FOR THE REST OF YOUR PIDDLING, INSIGNIFICANT LIFE!"

145

Right on cue, everyone in the room became rooted. Iorga crossed the room and walked around us, inspecting us like we were statues. I tried. I couldn't move a muscle. Iorga walked up to Case and slapped his face, forehand and backhand several times.

"GET USED TO IT, STINKY," he said. "I THINK I'M GOING TO MAKE YOU MY COURT JESTER. HOW WOULD YOU LIKE IT IF EVERYTHING YOU SAID WAS A SUREFIRE BELLY LAUGH? I KNOW SOME TV COMEDIANS WHO WOULDN'T MIND THAT A BIT. WHAT DO YOU SAY, STINKY?"

"I'll kill you for this, Rodriguez," said Case between his teeth.

Suddenly, Case's desperate statement struck me as hilarious. I began to giggle, like a child. I looked around me. We were all laughing uncontrollably.

"Stop it! Stop it!" shouted Case. We couldn't help ourselves. It only made us laugh harder. Case was close to tears of rage and frustration now.

"You've got to stop!" cried Case, tears running down his cheeks.

There were tears running down my face too. Tears of laughter. Myra and I, turned loose from Eddie's grip, leaned on each other to stay upright. We were helpless with laughter. As useless as if Iorga/Eddie had still commanded us to be motionless. Then, suddenly as it had come, the gales of hilarity stopped. Before our eyes, Iorga/Eddie seemed to grow taller. He was now well over six feet tall!

"ENOUGH!" his telepathic voice rumbled. "I MUST NOW ADDRESS THOSE IDIOTS WAITING FOR MY PEARLS OF WISDOM. I HAVE SPECIAL PLANS FOR ALL OF YOU. IT WILL BEGIN WITH YOUR HAVING TO

WATCH ME PROCLAIMED THE NEW MESSIAH. TO-
NIGHT, I SHALL RAISE THE DEAD, CURE THE LAME,
THE HALT, AND THE BLIND. I WILL FEED THE MULTI-
TUDES AND LEAD THEM IN THE PATH OF RIGH-
TEOUSNESS. THEY WILL ADORE AND WORSHIP
ME. AS WELL THEY SHOULD, FOR I AM GOD. YOU
FOOLS WILL WATCH IT ALL. FOR A REAL FLASH
ENDING, I AM GOING TO ASCEND INTO HEAVEN. I
WILL RISE A HUNDRED FEET ABOVE THE STA-
DIUM'S UPPERMOST TIER. THEN AS THEY ALL
WATCH AND PRAY, I WILL DISAPPEAR IN A FLASH
OF HOLY, BLINDING LIGHT. THEY WILL ALL HEAR
MY EXALTED VOICE SAY, 'I SHALL RETURN TO YOU,
MY CHILDREN.' "

Rodriguez/Iorga stopped and laughed again. "I HAVE
TO RETURN, OF COURSE. I HAVE TWO MORE BIG,
BIG SHOWS TO DO AT THIS PLACE. THAT'S THE
WAY TO DO IT, MYRA, DEAR. YOU WERE RIGHT. I
MISCALCULATED IN TRYING TO RULE THE EARTH
BY FORCE THE LAST TIME. IT'S REALLY TRUE. LOVE
CONQUERS WHERE THE SWORD FAILS. NA-
TURALLY, I HAVE SWORD READY IF THE FAITH-
FUL DON'T MOVE ON CUE. BUT IT'S TIME NOW. WE
MUST GO. "I AM READY, SWING WIDE THE
GATES!" he thundered.

It took me a second to realize that he wasn't address-
ing our little group. He was speaking to the group of
lackeys waiting anxiously outside the dressing room
door. It swung open. Sister Evelyn was just outside. She
held up a heavily embroidered cloak. The overhead
lights in the corridor, dim as they were, caused small
rainbow reflections to dance across the walls and ceiling.

"NOT NOW, MY DEAR," said Iorga aloud to Sister Evelyn. "NOT UNTIL I'M ON THE PLATFORM." Iorga turned and strode down the corridor. As though we were puppets, we turned and followed him.

"YOU WILL ALL BE ON THE PLATFORM," he "said" to us. "I WANT YOU TO SEE ME ASSUME MY TRUE GODHEAD."

We walked a few more blocks in silence. I could already hear the capacity crowd in the stands. The roar shook the great stadium to its foundations as we all emerged blinking into the bright lights that illuminated the infield area. It became even greater as the crowd saw Iorga/Eddie. We ascended the stairs to the platform. I didn't think it possible, but when Iorga waved his hands in benediction, the entire throng fell silent. You could have heard a flea kicking a cotton ball around.

"MY CHILDREN," he began. I gave a shudder, and then he launched into his scenario, exactly as he'd told us he would.

Suddenly, as though a candle flame had been blown out, the stadium and the lights all disappeared! I looked about me. Myra, Case, Bakka, Jacobs and Carbone were all still seated where they had been, on folding chairs. I looked below me and my stomach wrenched. We were suspended in utter emptiness!

No, wait. As our eyes became accustomed to the dimness, they appeared. The stars! Billions upon billions of them. I saw constellations I vaguely recognized. But they were subtly changed. The Big Dipper was askew. Then I realized that the constellations were the same. It was my point of observation that was different. Far away, who knows how far, there was a melon-sized object of bright, piercing light. We were close to some star; which one I couldn't say.

I felt no chill. I know that deep space is airless, yet I could breathe normally. I know that deep space is soundless, yet I clearly heard THE VOICE. It was at once the most awe-inspiring and infinitely comforting sound I have ever heard. It said, *"Turn, Ianos Iorga, and meet your destruction!"*

Iorga wheeled and looked at the same time we all did. Then we saw *him.* Have you ever seen Michelangelo's *David?* The figure before us was immense, yet so exquisitely formed. It was completely nude, save for an aura of coruscating light that seemed to illuminate the entire cosmos. I would have, were there not empty space beneath my feet, left my chair and fallen to my knees. The grandeur, the incomparable cosmic majesty of the figure before us, was humbling, yet somehow strangely exalting. Then in a flash, I realized why this godlike figure seemed familiar. If he had been cast in the mold of a god, the figure was Luis Jesús Ortiz!

I turned to see Iorga, and my blood changed to water. He too was growing in size. A similar aura, pale green, was crackling about his figure as it grew and . . . changed.

I felt bitter bile rise from my stomach and began to gag as I saw the form that was Ianos Iorga or Eddie Rodriguez change. Into something I recognized as well. Something loathsome. He was the nightmare that man has tried to depict since he first began to scratch on cave walls with a bit of charred wood and primitive pigments. The taloned fingers, the slimy scales, and the eyes that glowed like two red spots of perdition itself.

"I HAVE WAITED FOR THIS TIME!" the ghastly form

149

roared. "I HAVE WAITED OVER THE MILLENNIA, SA-
VORING THE TASTE THAT THIS MOMENT WOULD
BRING. WE ARE OLD FOES, YOU AND I." The obscene
figure licked its lips as a dribble of greenish fluid ran
down the left corner of its cavernous mouth.

"*As I have for you,*" said the Luis-thing. "*I remember
too well. I knew you as Aries when we were both children. I have known you as Temuchin and as Caligula.
I have know you as Attila and Hitler. And I know you
for what you have always been since the time we first
struggled at this very spot. I know you, Lucifer!*"

"AS I HAVE KNOWN YOU AS APOLLO, RA,
CHRIST, BUDDHA, AND ALLAH. NOW, KNOW MY
WRATH!"

The huge dark figure made a motion with its hand.
A bolt of energy so bright that it blinded me flowed
forth. Space itself vibrated and the cosmos grew dark.
A white glow enveloped the glorious figure that reminded me of Luis. I felt a rush of heat. The white aura
around the godlike shape began to shift spectrally. It
changed color from deep violet to dull red, as the hor-
rid shape sent bolt after bolt at the form. Nearby,
though it must have been billions of miles away, a star
burst into nova.

To my horror, I saw the godlike handsome figure
begin to grow smaller. IT was winning! The fury of raw
energy that dwarfed suns crackled and coursed around
us. The godlike figure grew still smaller, the shifting
aura about it now only glowing fitfully. The obscene
thing that had been Iorga screamed in triumph.

"FEEL IT!" it screamed in unholy glee. "FEEL AND
KNOW MY POWER, YOU INTERFERING MEDDLER.
YOU SINGER OF PSALMS, YOU PIOUS PIECE OF

150

OFFAL! KNOW THE POWER OF MY BEING AND TREMBLE! YOU WILL WORSHIP ME WITH ALL THE REST. FEEL IT AND KNOW FEAR!"

Deep space crackled and roared. The light around the diminishing figure grew fainter, then finally winked out. For a second, there was a hush, then again, that awful, obscene laughter. I felt my bowels empty with fear as the creature turned its glowing gaze upon us.

"AND NOW, FOR MY PLANET!" the huge obscenity roared. "IT WAS ALWAYS MINE. BEFORE THAT PIOUS ASS INTERFERED. AND IT IS AGAIN MINE!"

"Then turn again, Lucifer!"

I didn't see the form at first. No one could have. Its immensity blotted out the stars and the sun that I had seen nearby. It seemed to fill space itself. It dwarfed the cosmos, and a great hand reached down. It picked up the evil *thing* as though it were a child's doll.

"You will never again threaten this world of creatures I love," it said. *"I will have done with you this time."*

"MERCY!" screamed the dwarf-like shape in that immense hand. "I WILL OBEY YOU! I WILL BE YOUR SERVANT AGAIN! YOUR MOST LOVING AND FAITHFUL SERVANT." The figure squirmed and ran helplessly across the vast palm that held it in its hollow. As the tiny figure screamed for mercy, the hand slowly began to close into a fist!"OH, PLEASE!" the Iorga-thing cried. "I COULD HAVE DESTROYED YOUR FOLLOWERS, YOUR CHURCHES. I DIDN'T! MERCY, PLEASE. PLEASE!"

The great hand hesitated, then began to unfold.

"GOOD, GOOD!" cried the evil thing in its grasp. "YOU WON'T REGRET IT. I PROMISE. YOU HAVE MY SOLEMN WORD!"

151

"From the prince of all lies," said the immense figure, smiling.

"NO, NO! IT WILL BE DIFFERENT THIS TIME. I PROMISE!"

"Then remember your promise," said the figure. It picked up the devil-thing between thumb and forefinger and with a casual flick, sent it spinning toward the distant, melon-sized star. Its cry faded in an eerie Doppler effect as it tumbled over and over, disappearing finally into the dark of deep space.

As the retreating figure diminished in size, so did the vast, godlike thing. Finally, it was no more than twenty feet above us. It looked down on us and smiled. I felt an air of well-being surround me. I felt a joy so intense and indescribable that, to this day, I think back on it and try to recapture it. But in vain.

"I will return you now, children," it said. *"Do not be afraid."*

It made a motion with its hand. In that instant, we were all back on the platform in Yankee Stadium. Ianos Iorga still had his hands raised in benediction. It was as though time itself had stopped for the titanic battle way out there. Everything frozen.

Then slowly, as the great crowd at the stadium watched, Iorga's hands gradually dropped to his sides. A look of utter bewilderment crossed his face. It rapidly turned to apprehension. He couldn't have known he was speaking into an open microphone. He spun his gaze all about him, open panic visible on his features. He spoke a sentence in another language. It seemed Slavic, with Latin overtones. I assumed he was speaking in Rumanian. It turned out later I was right. It translates as, "Where am I? Who are all these people?"

152

Then he spied Father Carbone on the platform. He rushed over and threw himself at Carbone's feet. He spoke again in Rumanian. I guess Carbone had been chosen for his job because he spoke back to him in the same tongue. We all looked askance at the little priest.

"He is asking me to save him," smiled Carbone. "He's frightened of the crowds and the lights."

As Carbone and the frightened Iorga conversed in rapid Rumanian, the huge crowd began to get restless. If they knew what was going on, what had happened, it would have meant a panic. Possibly a riot. I don't know where I got the presence of mind. I walked up to the microphone and addressed the crowd.

At first, I didn't get across. I was speaking too fast. Echo after echo rolled through the many speakers in the stadium and turned my words to gibberish. The crowd grew more restive. I slowed down and said, "Ladies and gentlemen. Brother Ianos has been taken suddenly ill. We must take him to get aid. Please clear a path."

The words worked beautifully. As we strolled across the infield, the mass of humanity parted to let us pass. We quickly made our way below. Bless George Case. With Eddie gone, he could see again. The situation was one he recognized. He was immediately in command. He got on a walkie-talkie and in no time had a squad of men around us. We waited until most of the crowd was gone upstairs. Once it had thinned out, Case ordered a helicopter to the infield of the stadium. We quickly boarded. Shortly, we were all seated in the suite reserved for VIPs at the Waldorf-Astoria Towers, courtesy of the Dakaman government.

Ianos Iorga, who understood nothing of what was

153

going on, was taken off somewhere by Case's men. Myra told Case that he could just as easily let Iorga go. He's harmless now. The Eddie-thing is no longer inside him. But as Myra put it, "Case is a Secret Policeman. They like to lock people up. Whether they are dangerous or not."

The Dakaman Ambassador was exultant. He ordered some of the Waldorf's very best champagne. It didn't seem to bother him that, when it arrived, only he and I drank some. The rest of our group were all non-drinkers. When he found out, he smiled broadly and said, "A pity, Dr. Grossman, that we are surrounded by non-imbibers. I'm afraid we must make the supreme sacrifice and drink this magnum of *Dom Pérignon* all by ourselves." We raised our glasses. "Ladies and gentlemen," continued Selim Bakka. "I give you the benefactor of our cause: that incredible god we met, whatever its name may be."

"Gee, thanks, guys," said a voice. And we all glanced up to see Luis Ortiz standing in the doorway!

Selim Bakka

The way Ortiz explains it, none of us ever left the platform in Yankee Stadium. And each of us saw a different thing when Ortiz fought Iorga. I know that I saw *Yag*, the god of my childhood defeat, Grif, the father of all demons. Case saw Christ wrestle with the Devil. It seems that whatever we wished to see, each of us saw.

We spent a few hours comparing notes as to what

each of us did see. Ortiz says we all saw the truth. According to how one perceives truth. The only one who said nothing of what she saw was Dr. Sokolow. And I truly wonder what it was *she* saw.

I am going to resign my post here at the U.N. I no longer have the need to hold this appointment. I am going to return to my own country. And I shall be Prime Minister. I realize now that the forces of darkness can only take hold of power if good men stand idly by and allow it to happen. The people of the back country will have their voice. But I do wonder just what it was that Dr. Sokolow saw.

Martin Grossman

Bermuda is a lovely island. The sand is pink, the sky is blue. And the ocean is warm. It's true there isn't much to do after you've seen the shows at the hotels. And often, they're even the same performers, working each hotel in succession. It is, however, a perfect spot for a honeymoon. Myra and I are very content.

The YPI Church still exists, but I estimate that in another year's time, the last of it will be gone. The key members Iorga/Eddie had under his influence were the first to go. Edward Saunders has withdrawn financial support of the church and disappeared again. They say he's in Costa Rica. I couldn't care less.

Case gave me the best wedding present I could have, a complete release from my obligation to the I.G.O.

Selim Bakka gave us a diamond the size of a robin's egg from the back country mines in his land.

The best gift of all came from Luis Ortiz. He's happy now too. Or as happy as an inquiring mind like his can be. He's dropped the school program at M.I.T. Says there's no need to study what you already know. When I asked what he intended to do with the rest of his life, he smiled and said, "First, I am going to make my father the happiest man in East Hampton. I am going into the wholesale Spanish grocery business."

I was aghast. I began protesting that he has a responsibility to his incredible talents.

"Sure, sure," he said with a wave of his hand. "But I'm just sixteen. My dad is middle-aged. I can give him happiness for the rest of his life and still have a young lifetime left. The power won't go away."

"Then what will you do?" Myra asked.

"I don't know," Luis said. "I may pay a visit to the Dalai Lama. He's quite lonely, you know. But before I go, let me do this for you, Martin."

I felt the strangest sensation. As though a cold hand was reaching inside my brain. It felt as though someone were opening a door, casting a bright light on the shadows within.

"There, Martin," said Luis with a grin. "How's that?"

At first, I felt no difference. Then perception of what Luis had done swept across me like a sunrise on the Atlantic. We were standing at the boarding gate at Kennedy Airport, ready to take our flight to Bermuda. Instantly, I became aware of the babble of thoughts around me. The airlines clerk at the desk had a stomach-ache. The woman boarding ahead of us was going to see her daughter in Bermuda. She was quite happy about it. The man next to her was terribly depressed. Almost suicidal.

Then I turned to Myra. For the first time in our lives we communicated. Utterly, fully. Mind to mind. Soul to soul, if you prefer. Luis had bestowed the gift upon me!

Luis embraced and kissed Myra. Then he abruptly walked away. The boarding line began to move, and we all broke into that sheeplike shuffle airline passengers use when boarding a plane through those mobile gates. I took Myra's hand as we walked. I could no longer see Luis Ortiz. But as we were shown to our seats, I heard his mental voice again. "By the way Martin," it said. "Do you still remember all the words to *Marching Through Georgia?*"

Rafael Guzman

I missed Eddie by only a few hours. I went to the apartment in Sheepshead Bay, and there was this letter waiting for me. He used the place on Friday and Saturday nights. I hadda take care of the store, and be with Luisa over the weekend. What rotten luck! I ain't seen Eddie in over three years.

But to show you what kind of a class guy Eddie Rodriguez is, you should see the letter he left for me. But nobody's gonna see it, not even Luisa when we get married. I'm gonna keep it with my other things from Eddie. In my stash. I read it so often now, I could burn the letter and still remember what it says, though.

Dear Rafael,

Sorry I couldn't stick around and get together with you. I didn't have time to straighten up the place before I left, either. I was only here Friday and Saturday nights, even then for only a few hours. And I won't be coming back for a long, long time. Maybe never.

But the apartment, *hermano,* is all yours. I had you use the name Ortiz because I didn't want anyone to know where I was staying. It was also a joke on somebody that didn't come off.

It's no joke that it's yours, though. The lease paper is on the kitchen table, and I signed it over to you. Now you can marry Luisa Quinones. Oh yeah, I know about that. *Buena suerte, hermano, y hasta la vista.*

Eddie

See what I mean about class? A whole place full of stuff straight outa Bloomingdales. For a wedding present. Wish I coulda seen him, though. But I think, somehow, I'm gonna cross paths with Eddie Rodriguez again. He said so in his letter. He didn't say good-bye, he said *hasta la vista.* And in my book, that means, "Until I see you again." Gee, I can hardly wait . . .

Glossary

Buena suerte, hermano, y hasta la vista   Good luck, brother, until I see you again.

demonio (m.)   Demon

gringo (m.)   English-speaking man

hermano (m.)   Brother

Latino (m.)   Latin person

Noli me tangere, Satanas   Do not touch me, Satan.

¿Que tal?   How are you?

sinvergüenza (m. and f. pl.)   scoundrels